THE BREAD OF EXILE

THE BREAD OF EXILE

A NOVEL

by

KAREN GERSHON

LONDON

VICTOR GOLLANCZ LTD

1985

First published in Great Britain 1985
by Victor Gollancz Ltd,
14 Henrietta Street, London WC2E 8QJ

British Library Cataloguing in Publication Data
Gershon, Karen
The bread of exile.
I. Title
823'.914[F]   PR6057.E7
ISBN 0-575-03599-4

Photoset by Centracet
Printed in Great Britain by
St Edmundsbury Press, Bury St Edmunds, Suffolk

For my grandchildren

CONTENTS

ONE

DECEMBER 1938

(Dovercourt)

IT WAS ONLY for them that the day broke unlike any other.

In the night it had snowed, not so much as to transform all the world into a children's playground, but enough to establish beyond doubt that they were the first people out and about in their street, the boy thought as he looked over his shoulder at his footprints. His sister at once looked over her shoulder, too: she had decided to copy, from now on, everything he did: he was her one remaining certainty.

The children, aged fifteen and thirteen, were carrying their suitcases themselves: there was nothing left which their parents could do for them. The mother had still had her uses, even that morning: for the last time setting the table for four—though none of them could make themselves eat anything. When she had, for the last time, redrawn the parting in her daughter's long dark hair, her son had come forward and presented his mop-head, too: bowing it to hide his face from her and to let her get at it, being already taller than she though not by much. But the father, who had long ago ceased to be able to provide for his family, and could no longer protect it, had failed even in his bid to do his son one last favour.

In the passport office, he had asked, "Is it possible for the boy to change his name?" He had spoken quietly and firmly, as if he were not taking an outrageous risk, and stood there dignified and apparently unshaken—his bearing, his son thought, diminishing all the uniformed officials—throughout the uproar which he had provoked: because the boy's name happened to be Adolf—though he had been Dolph to all who knew him long before the world had heard of Hitler. Was the Führer's name not good enough for his son? "He is going to England and it's not an

English name." The argument was Dolph's, who cursed himself when he heard his father repeat it: men were being sent to concentration camps for less. The brownshirt asked him if he were afraid of being mistaken for a member of the Hitler Youth? "Don't worry, son, your passport will make it plain for all to see that you're a Yid." The English knew how to deal with the Jews, he told him, they had burned Jews and synagogues long before there was a German Reich; Dolph knew only of the twelfth-century pogrom in York. He had explained to his sister, who always believed what he said, that England did not want them either though it was offering Jewish children a temporary refuge: opening its gates with its left hand to salve its conscience for almost closing, with its right, the gates of Palestine; brother and sister had straw hats to wear against the eastern sun among their belongings. They were allowed to take out of Germany what they could carry in one suitcase, and half a mark.

Although they intended to journey so far away, it did not occur to Inge that she was walking through her home town together with her parents for the last time. She had heard them say, "When people return to places they knew as children, they find them smaller," and, "When people meet adults they knew as children, they find them younger," and thus without being lied to was deceived into believing that she would one day come back and find them again, that it was not necessary, in order to have more of life, to give anything up: as she would not have to give up her knowledge of German in order to learn English. That was how she came to be hurrying up the hill to the station ahead of the others until her brother called out, "You've demonstrated that you can march with your suitcase!" It made her wish that she were going alone. Later, she always hoped that he had succeeded in making their parents believe that that was what she had been doing: that they had not known how impatient she had been for what was coming next.

It cannot have been much too early for the first tram: there were people waiting for it, some of them reading, by the snow-brightened light of the street lamp, the anti-Semitic *Stürmer* newspaper displayed at every stop. They watched the family passing by—Jews were no longer allowed to use the trams—perhaps as cows watch what crosses their pasture; but Inge still had illusions about her own importance. And in fact one man stepped forward and barred their way, less with his physical presence than by serving as a reminder that Jews were no longer allowed to use the pavements. The mother looked at her children and moved over into the gutter. "Please!" the man said to the father. "Let me carry the little ones' suitcases!" Their father had come to the town—their mother's native town—after four years in the German trenches; he had old comrades and masonic brothers everywhere, even among the Nazis. But he did not know this man; he turned to his son with a gesture that consulted him and Dolph thought, they throw me out, and then they want me to make them feel better about it? But what he said was, "We'll carry our own suitcases;" he even added, "thank you!" He took a step forward and the man stood aside for him, and told him in a voice loud enough for others to hear, "I want you to know that one German at least is ashamed of what is being done to you!" Later, the boy tried to explain to his sister that the man had said it not for their sake but his own; she would have argued about it but she could no longer afford to think that her brother might be in the wrong: she had to be able to rely on him as absolutely as, at the time of that other exodus, Moses had relied on God. Afterwards the boy thought that he ought to have obliged the man, for the sake of his father who still thought of himself as a German.

Because the mother would not come back on to the pavement, the other three also walked along in the gutter.

She was small and fat and dressed in the mourning she had been wearing for the past five and a half years, her parents having been among Hitler's first victims: when her father, president of the Jewish community, had been taken into "protective custody", her mother had committed suicide and he had not long survived her death, and his own imprisonment. Now, as they arrived where there were crowds of people, she gave up the pretence that she was not weeping; her children looked at each other with more embarrassment than pity.

To them, the station was a magical place: producing over the years at erratic intervals unpredictable aunts and uncles and, once, a whole family: their father's brothers and sisters and their children on the way from Berlin, where he had been born, to some spa in the Rhineland; they stopped long enough to provide a restaurant meal and—never able to remember the ages of their brother's children—unsuitable presents. How was it that they could still manage, Frau Stein asked her husband, who called them crooks because they were middlemen; though he himself, who had been an architect (some of the best modern buildings in the town were his, including a real showpiece), had recently been reduced to peddling pocket calculators among his acquaintances. "I'm earning my place in Hitler's heaven for Jews," he told his children, his ebony eyes twinkling; Dolph had inherited both their colour and their twinkle.

At the end of every synagogue service, their rabbi admonished, "Go home quickly in twos and threes, avoid attracting attention, don't congregate!" That morning the station was full of Jews: parents who had brought their children and too few organisers: a month after the burning of the synagogue, most of the heads of the community were either dead or in Dachau. Herr Stein was at once asked to go to the platform where—no parents allowed—a hysterical mother was in trouble with the police. Inge, seeing him leaving her—though in the direction in which she would be going—plunged after him and caught him by the belt of his coat. He saw that she had abandoned her suitcase, reassured her and told her to wait for her brother. She turned round and, seeing him and her mother with their arms about each other, tried to get back to them through the turnstile and the people between who were either moving her way or were there for the purpose of preventing her going back. She tried to explain that she had not yet said good-bye to her mother, but it came out as a wail of, "Mutti! Mutti!" which made other children on her side of the barrier pause; Dolph was to say that it had looked as if they would all stampede back. Seeing his sister manhandled by the brownshirts, he too plunged through; their two suitcases had to be passed along to them. But Inge, when her brother turned out not to be for but against her, would have fought him as well, if he had not said, "That whistle is our train about to leave!" It was the first lie he had ever told her. It was harder for him, who was old enough to understand what was happening to them.

They neither of them said good-bye to their father, who

appeared near the rear of the train as it drew out, and they were in the carriage next to the engine. "Don't run!" they shouted together; the previous year he had suffered a heart-attack. He did not look like a man within three years of his death, did not look like one humbled, persecuted, bereft: but rather like Samson about to take hold of the pillars.

That was only the local train, which took them to Hamm, or it may have been Dortmund, to catch the train which, starting in Vienna, had been gathering Jewish refugee children from all over Greater Germany on its way. As they were changing platforms, the handle broke on Inge's suitcase, which was new but shoddy, the best they had been able to afford. She could not carry it like that and they swopped cases, but she could not manage to carry Dolph's case for more than a few steps at a time; they could not keep up with the group to which they belonged. They saw it boarding the train further along the platform.

"This will do," Dolph said. "It's marked *reserved*," Inge pointed out. "For us, little idiot!" He was short of breath and red in the face, still manfully battling with his boy's emotions. She did not doubt his word but wondered how he knew and, looking up, saw the children at the windows or rather, she saw one face: that of an adult-looking boy, rather handsome, watching them with raised eyebrows. Meeting her eyes, he turned away—disgusted, she thought, by the spectacle which she and her brother presented. But he was waiting for them at the carriage door and took her suitcase; by the time she reached the compartment it had already been put up on the rack. All the seats except one were taken, all by boys. "There are two of us," Dolph said. The boy who had come to help him in gazed at him, and then at Inge, and exclaimed, "How charming, Hansel and Gretel!" He beamed at them, and motioned to the boys on the other bench to make space. "I would give up my own seat for your sister," he said to Dolph, "but that would rather defeat the purpose of bringing you in here to keep me company."

He sat down opposite them as the train began to move, and looked out of the window, as if to give them time to take him in: his hair was black and would have been curly if it had not been brilliantined into wavelets, his eyes looked quite black they were

13

so deeply-set; he had the slightly rounded nose and rather full mouth which were being ceaselessly caricatured in the *Stürmer*. He was elegant in a pepper-and-salt knickerbocker suit with many pockets and with leather buttons. A matching cap lay on a pigskin case above his head. Brother and sister exchanged a look: they were impressed by him. His name was Rudi.

"Mine's David," Dolph said, and shook hands with him. Inge introduced herself and they both shook hands all round. Rudi had been to England before, he had relations in London who were acting as his guarantors—all the children had to have guarantors, but for most of them these were the multiplicity of English people who had contributed their pennies to the funds of the Movement for the Care of Children from Germany. Rudi, too, had only a transit visa, but he thought that his relations would be able to arrange for him to stay; he already knew English and meant to go to university, either Oxford or Cambridge. "You're lucky," Dolph said, and Rudi smiled at him and said, "What's lucky is that I paid a farewell visit to Berlin or I wouldn't have been on this train because my home is in Hamburg." He gave him a meaningful look and Dolph looked at Inge, to make it register with her that he was being treated as an equal by one already so adult and independent; they both thought that Rudi had meant that it was lucky for them that he was on their train. It was their turn to explain that they were Youth Aliyah wards. Dolph said, "I promised my mother not to let her out of my sight—" which was obviously absurd and news to Inge—"until I can hand her over to the children's village of Ben Shemen." His own destination was kibbutz Deganiah. "But I shall stop to look at Jerusalem on the way." Never before having travelled, it was the best he could do. They knew more Hebrew than English and, at that time, when they spoke of home they meant not Germany or their native town but at most the flat in which they had lived with their parents, or else they meant Palestine.

Some of the boys were bound for the United States. They had not yet got through stating their destinations when the door of the compartment was opened by a young woman with a sharp and tired face, who exclaimed, to Inge, "What are you doing in here among the boys? Come out, little minx, in with the girls for you!" Inge took hold of her brother's hand and thought, they will have to chop me off at the wrist to get me away from him! and felt her heart flooding as he returned the pressure. He said, "She is my sister!" sounding proud of her; it was to be more than two years before he confessed to her how close to tears he had been brought by the sudden realization that she was all that was left to him of his childhood.

"But you're not babies!" the woman exclaimed, with a baleful look at Rudi who, the oldest one there, was not yet seventeen, the upper age limit for the children's transports. They ought not to make problems for the people who were helping them! She stood there muttering about selfishness and ingratitude; to the children it sounded as if she were cursing them and Dolph asked, with an ominous calmness, "Are we not through yet with being told where we may and where we may not sit?" which prompted someone to call out to her, "Nazi!" The woman's face crumpled as she turned away and Dolph, to whom it had not occurred before that she would have her problems, too, stood up at once and drew Inge out into the corridor. "Not being able to have things your own way doesn't mean that you have to give up altogether," he began to educate her for their refugee status.

They had to let go of each other when the track curved, to hold on. After a while he asked her, "What did you put in?"

In the days of their true childhood, they had each had their own room, and all it occurred to their parents they might want; but for the past five years they had been sharing a bedroom, which their mother had partitioned with a curtain, transparent and not reaching up to the ceiling as there was only the one window at Dolph's end. Last night they had not drawn it because most likely they would never again share a room. He told her, "I couldn't sleep either, I saw you take out your new grey sweater." It had not been new but had come out of one of the charity bundles which had been clothing them for years, though their mother had somehow always managed to buy them their shoes. They had each been packing and re-packing their one suitcase for days, often with their mother standing over them, pausing in her weeping to tell them not to leave out clothes for the sake of other things: games, keepsakes, but especially books. Most of their books they had sold, and bought box cameras with the proceeds; some they had had to burn for fear of a house search by the Gestapo. "I wanted one of my bears," Inge said, while Dolph was wondering whether to tell her that he had some contraband: favourite pages he had saved from the banned authors, a complete chapter from Gorki's *Mother*. His selection of Heine's poems he had kept whole, as a reminder, should he ever need one, that he was no coward: Heine had got him thrown out of school at the age of thirteen when he had put him forward as the author of the *Lorelei*, that favourite German song; though the true reason for his expulsion had been that, while he was there and top of the class, his chief rival, the son of a Gauleiter, would never be able to do better than come second.

It surprised him that he should wish to burden his little sister with his own apprehension; he told himself that weaknesses in one's character did not matter as long as one was aware of them and could be on one's guard. He could not say this to Inge: she would think that he was implying that there was something wrong with *her*. He felt sorry for her for now having no one except him, and sorry for himself for not having even a Dolph—and was suddenly impatient to get back to the other boys, to whom he could say whatever came into his head, because he was not responsible for them and they could like him or lump him. The next compartment was one which was full of girls. "Why don't you go in there for a bit?" he asked Inge—and felt it like a slap in the face when she did: to prove to him that she had sense enough not to take his promise to their mother literally.

The customs men (if that was what they were), Rudi told him, would not be interested in finding anything: the Germans wanted to be rid of them, didn't they? He said, "If you're having second thoughts and want to throw something out of the window, we'll all look the other way. Alternatively, you may put it in among my things, since you have a sister to take care of and I have no one. I won't even ask what it is." But while Dolph was still wondering whether the offer was meant to be accepted, or had been made merely to let him know that here was a friend, Rudi asked him, "Is it communist stuff?" Dolph blushed to have been so overestimated, but knowing that a lie would put an end to what was beginning between them, he said, "Not really. Poetry mostly." Rudi laughed. "I might have known! With your looks!" which were romantic and had made even the brownshirt in the passport office call him, son.

They had anticipated the crossing of the border out of Germany as the greatest experience in their anguished lives, but missed it, busy repacking: the contents of their suitcases had been, without being looked at, emptied on to the floor, their belongings had been mixed up—and their hands were still shaking. Inge felt tempted to disown her bear until she saw Rudi handling it as if it were his own; he even spoke to it, uncondescendingly, while helping her to fit it in. Another boy fixed the broken handle. When their cases were back on the racks, they all sat smiling, feeling intimately acquainted, feeling willing to lay down their lives for each other. And then they were in Holland.

The platform was crowded with people, mainly women, who had oranges and bars of chocolate and cocoa in cardboard beakers which they handed up through the windows; laughing or weeping, they called out, "Welcome! We bid you welcome!" in Dutch and German and, some, in English. "God bless you!" they shouted. "Dolph—" Inge began to ask, but it was Rudi who was leaning out over her shoulder, softly saying, "Look at that! Look at that! Look at that!" Even following his eyes, she was left wondering what he found so amazing: except that there were no Nazi uniforms, no swastika flags and no portraits of Hitler, they might have been at any station in northern Germany.

The Dutch had paid a supplement so that the children could cross the Channel with berths to sleep in, as if they were tourists. As far as Inge was concerned, they had not done them a favour: she could, just then, think of nothing more romantic than spending the night on deck under the shifting stars, on the lookout for the white cliffs—in the company of her brother.

Not only was she separated from him, she did not know where he was: if fire broke out or the ship went down or the boys were disembarked separately, she would never find him again among all those people and regulations and orders given in English which she did not understand. She took her bear to bed with her, not caring what the other girls thought; when she was sick in the night it was taken away; perhaps she could have got it back if she had asked about it: she didn't because she believed that its loss was God's punishment for deceiving her mother.

For almost as long as she could remember, her family had been planning to emigrate: to Palestine, to the Argentine, to Siam, to Shanghai; nothing had come of her father's endeavours because he had no capital and was only an architect—it would have been better, he often said, if he had been a bricklayer; not until after his heart attack had the parents given in to their children and agreed to let them go, on their own, to Palestine. England had never been thought of as a possible destination: it had been sprung on them no more than three weeks before when, after the *Kristallnacht*, it offered itself as a wayside station. They had tried to prepare themselves by looking at the illustrations in their Dickens novels and Sherlock Holmes stories, before selling them. On the maps in their school atlas England in relation to the rest of the world had been so small that Inge had half expected to be able to look across and see the ocean on the other side. There were no white cliffs because they had landed at Harwich.

Dolph, as she might have known, had charmed some sailor into showing him all over the ship including the engine room; she ran into Rudi, also looking for him. He did not show up until the loudspeakers started ordering them about, and then stood there in the double line with his nose in the air, refusing to be drawn into a quarrel. But he held on to Inge's hand so tightly that the feel of it stayed with her for life; he let go only once: to hang a cardboard label on a piece of string about her neck; the number it bore came next to his and made her believe that they would not be separated.

There are photographs of these children landing in England, though who would have thought at that time that even Jewish *children* in Germany were in danger of their lives: they believed that they had come because their parents could no longer feed and clothe them, could no longer ensure their schooling or protect them from being attacked in the streets. There were reporters on the quayside who spoke to those who had some English, but Rudi soon withdrew from that group, shaking his head. "They think we're just making it up," he said. "One asked me, had we come in order to cause trouble between our two countries?"

They were standing in line for the buses to take them to the reception camp at Dovercourt, when it started to snow. "Do you think it is snowing in Germany, too?" sister asked brother. He let go of her hand to adjust her hood, and then turned his back on her. That told her, more plainly than his face would have done, that he was thinking the neighbours will ring the doorbell and shout, come on Jew, shovel the snow! and how can Papa do it with his wonky heart? Did I expect Mutti to do it? I ought never to have left them! She scratched at the small of his back, hard, to let him feel it through his *Loden* coat, and he turned round not because he wanted her but because he wanted the rest of the world even less.

Rudi came running along the line, looking for them; he pushed an envelope at Dolph. On the back was his London address—his name was on the list for the camp at Ipswich. "What shitty luck!" Dolph exclaimed and Rudi gazed at him, his face brightening as he asked, "Do you mind? Do you truly mind?" A glance at Inge decided him that they needed cheering up. "Oi Hansel and Gretel, what is to become of you!" he declaimed, half stage Jew, half clown, and continued until he had got a smile out of them. He said, "Don't despair, children, depend on Rudi to put matters right!" and off he went, watched by their wistful eyes: he was the first warmth in their cold new lives.

They had more faith in him than they had in themselves, but they did not have enough, were already sitting in one of the buses when somebody nearer to the door called out, "There is a Rudi here looking for—" and was prompted to add their names. The bus was full; they were not allowed to get off; but they saw him, pink-faced and radiant, and before the engine started up heard him shouting something about the next bunk. Dolph returned to his place, thoughtfully: Rudi must be as desperate for them as they were for each other. He was thrown against Inge as the bus moved off and, sitting down, discovered that she was crying. "Did I hurt you?" he asked. "Honestly . . .", exasperation in his voice, in his heart hosannas for Rudi who was his friend. She did not deign to explain what should have been obvious to him: that he would be sharing a room with strangers, God knew how many light-years away from where she would be, and the mention of bunks had made her realize that not only would her mother no longer be there to kiss her good-night and good-morning, but even asleep she would be beset by the unfamiliar.

The snow had pitched in the fields and on the low hedgerows—and on the roofs of the wooden huts that were somewhat bigger but not very different from the sheds people have on their allotments; there were rows upon rows of them and between them the wind blew, salty from the sea. "Look!" the woman with the lists said, throwing open a door as upon her own handiwork. "How nice and cosy you'll be!" The wind blew in at the door and out of the cracks in the window-frames and the walls; inside it smelled of the sea, and of damp wool. Most of the huts had two sets of bunks in them. "Now tell me if you want to be together," the young woman said, "sisters or friends, we want you to be happy here!" Four went in here and two in there; now Inge cursed herself for having been too much Inge to make friends on the journey. The woman looked into another hut and said, "Just one in here—is there anyone on her own?" How lucky I am, Inge thought, coming forward: this was one of the huts for three and what was waiting for her was a single bed.

She opened her suitcase, saw the space where her bear should have been, and burst into tears. One of her absent room-mates was untidy; one had ranged some belongings on one of the window-sills, including a small china cat; Inge, wishing that it were hers, had the impulse to smash it—hardly noticed before it was suppressed. There was also a photograph of a hard-faced woman in a fussy hat; looking at it, she thought, fancy anyone thinking of her as Mutti! and could not bring herself even to unpack her pyjamas. She was still blinking when the door flew open on a small red-faced girl who exclaimed, "Home at last! It's taken me ages to find it, all the huts are the same!" She must be stupid, Inge thought, and saw that she was a hunchback, a freak: one of those whom Hitler wished to have exterminated. It was still some while before Inge understood that she also belonged into that category.

20

Her name was Annie and she talked non-stop, happily; Inge, resentfully pursuing her own thoughts, missed hearing most of what she was being told about the camp: the sea was at the bottom of the field, that was what the constant noise was: it was wild; the place was not meant for winter use, that was why it was so cold. But the hall was heated. "I'll show you," Annie said; despising her, Inge left the hut without taking her bearings and later got into a panic before she found it again.

The hall was as large as a railway station, with a row of stoves that unfroze you only if you climbed inside one of the wire-net guards, always hung with coats that steamed and made puddles: when it wasn't snowing it was raining. On that day, people were still unpacking the cooking pots and the china stored after the summer season, and more which had been either bought or donated because of the number of children being expected. On that day, the several hundred who were already there seemed few in all that space.

They had been allowed into England on condition that they would not stay, either for longer than two years or beyond the age of seventeen, whichever was the sooner. They were to leave the camp—to make space for others—as soon as possible; to decide their immediate future they were interviewed. When Dolph and Inge were told to present themselves together, they felt reassured by so much consideration; but the girl with the forms merely wanted—this she said in English—"to kill two birds with one stone." "Please?" Dolph asked her to repeat this: he was grimly gulping down knowledge of English. She was studying German at Cambridge University, she told them, making them feel apprehensive and inferior but meaning to put them at their ease; unwilling to go to Nazi Germany, she was hoping that spending the Christmas vacation in the camp would do something for her accent; there were a lot of student volunteers—all, with their purposefulness and their self-assurance seeming adult even to the older children. She exchanged a smile with Dolph, failed to make Inge smile back, and squared the forms on her clip-board.

The first hurdle to be taken was Dolph's name. When she had accepted him as David, she asked, "What class were you in at school?" It took some minutes to convince her that he was not "having her on"—this in English—when he said that during the past two years he had learned, first carpentry and then shoemaking, working in a bicycle factory in between. It sounded as if he had no staying-power and Inge signalled to him to explain that it was because of his Jewishness ... But the girl appeared to be pleased with him. "So you're really willing to do almost anything?"

Rudi had warned them: if war broke out, as seemed likely, they might well have to stay in England until it was over: they ought to think twice about what they let themselves in for. "That was different," Dolph said, glancing at Inge for support. "I mean to become an architect, like my father." Pencil poised, the girl with the forms stared at him. "I can't put that down! You must remember that you are a refugee!" Dolph-David turned his back on her.

With a smile, she appealed to his sister: she was finding that the girls were easier, but this one, with her studious look, probably wanted to be no less than a teacher. Inge, furious with her for what she had done to her brother, offered the first thing that came into her head, "I want to be a gardener." It brought a small explosion from her brother, what they later learned to call a raspberry. Did he expect her to admit that she wanted to be a poet? To say that needed more self-confidence than she felt at the best of times; the most she would ever say was that she meant to become a writer. The girl was enthusiastic. "I know just the place for you. A lovely boarding school where you can learn just that while completing your education." Inge did not calculate the cost of her sacrifice but asked, "And my brother can go there, too, to complete his education?"—"Well no," the girl said, speaking now as to an equal. "He's missed two years' schooling, you see, and he'd be studying in a foreign language, he'd never catch up."

"It won't be a foreign language," Dolph said, with his back to them. "I beg your pardon?" the girl asked, and he turned round, eyes brimming and lips bitten scarlet. "If I stay in this country, it won't be a foreign language, not for me either, not for ever. By the time I am thirty-one, you see," he said with that talent for salesmanship that has made Jews their fortunes through the centuries the world over, "I shall have been speaking English for longer than German and—"

"Don't kid yourself," the girl with the form said, "that you'll ever be anything but a foreigner to the English." They did not believe her.

"He's got a brilliant mind." Inge repeated what she had overheard their rabbi saying to their father after Dolph had been expelled. The girl looked at her watch—it was nearly lunchtime—and promised that he should have his intelligence tested. "If he is as bright as you say," she told Inge, now her ally, "somebody may be willing to pay for his schooling." Rudi had told them that it could be had free. "That may be," the girl agreed. "But he would need money to live on."

Rudi did not think much of their going to a trade school; he said, "For that you could have stayed in Germany."

Life in Dovercourt was dominated by the loudspeakers. At first the announcements were translated, but later it was the same with them as with the milk in the tea: the children were told that they must get used to it.

Inge exploited her lack of English to boycott camp life whenever it threatened to take her brother away from her. For instance at mealtimes they were not supposed to sit together, but separately at the tables appropriate to their ages, because of the English visitors willing to foster children who were wandering about to take their pick. "But we won't go separately, anyway," Dolph and Inge argued, when he was hauled out from among the girls or she from among the boys. She needed his familiarity to help her cope with kippers for breakfast, prunes and custard for dessert: the taste of England which she found revolting because she was not ready to be weaned from Germany. He ate up whatever she left, heroically, to spare them all being reminded of the starving Jewish children still at home with their parents who would have liked nothing better than to change places with them—who frequently would have liked nothing better either.

One day Inge borrowed from her brother a shirt and tie, which she wore with her track suit, and found a ski-helmet under which to hide her long hair; of course it caused hilarity among those who were in the secret, passed on until everyone at their table was laughing. Others began to laugh, for the pure joy of it, until the infection had spread throughout the hall; they laughed till they needed to wipe their eyes and most of them did not know what about. When Rudi came over, after the meal, and was told, he said, "You make as charming a boy as your brother," and put his hand under her chin so that he could look at her; it was such a caring gesture that she fell in love with him.

One day they were in the little hall, where the piano was being played by someone with a fatal talent, when the loudspeaker said, "A-dolf—" pronouncing the name as if there might also be a B-dolf—"Stein to the office! A-dolf Stein to the office!"— "Don't go!" Inge reminded him, meaning: if they want to send you somewhere without me; Rudi asked, "Would you like me to come with you?" Believing that he was being summoned to be told that his father had been put in a concentration camp, or had died of a heart attack, or that his parents had taken their lives in a suicide pact, Dolph looked as if he might faint and dumbly shook his head. "Then I'll take care of your little sister until you get back," Rudi said. But afterwards they decided to follow him, and waited for him outside the office, for a very long time, in vain.

Some Zionist party officials, including two future members of the first Israeli Knesset, had come from London to get the children who were on their way to Palestine to renounce their certificates in favour of others who were still in Germany; someone had given them Dolph's name as that of a potential leader. They took him into a corner of the big hall, and held out a form for him to sign, to set an example to the others. "I didn't leave my parents, I didn't leave Germany, to remain a wandering Jew," Dolph said. They knew that, they told him: he should go on *hachsharah*, to prepare himself for kibbutz life, until the couple of years he was allowed to spend in England were up. He would be all right whereas God knew what might not happen within another couple of years to the Jews left in Germany. He was dedicated to the Jewish cause? Then here was something he could do for it, right now. "Sign and we will guarantee," they said, "that you shall get to Eretz Israel, we need people like you there." Dolph asked, "And my little sister?" They would guarantee that she would get there, too. "I promised my mother to see her settled in Ben Shemen," Dolph said, signing with his face close to his hand, unable to mention his mother and stay dry-eyed.

It meant, he explained to his sister and his friend, that he and Inge would have to separate, here in England as they would have done in Palestine. She was not old enough to go on *hachsharah* and he could not now do anything else than that: he must organize the Zionist children in the camp and see that none of them were lost to the movement through the imposed delay, as they might be if they continued with regular schooling until they started to have ambitions for themselves. "Haven't you?" Rudi asked in a shocked voice, with raised eyebrows, and Dolph answered firmly, "If Eretz Israel needs me to be a farmer, then a farmer I shall be." Grinning he added, "Maybe it'll still need architects before I'm too old to study?"

Ever since joining the Zionists, Inge had thought of them as a sort of elite: people who made something positive out of their Jewishness instead of regarding it as a curse; the Zionist children in Dovercourt knew where they belonged, not from their identity papers but from their hearts, did not have to look at those around them for clues as to who they ought to become but had the inheritance of who they were in their blood. They did not think much of English culture as it was presented to them in Dovercourt, did not want to learn how to dance the Lambeth Walk, preferred dancing the *horrah*; instead of *Daisy, Daisy, give me your answer do . . .* , they sang love songs to their homeland. Especially on a Friday night, when they dressed in blue and white, Inge felt that they were the chosen; she felt the seal of God's approval set on her when it was she who stepped up to the *kiddush* table and lit the two Sabbath candles. Afterwards the rabbi, who travelled weekly from London but spoke German, preached, "Remember that other children might have come here in your place, you must always be grateful and strive to justify, through your lives, that you are the ones who were saved."

Not all the children in the camp were Jewish, or had been raised as Jews; perhaps it was for them, and for the non-Jews among the volunteer staff, that a Christmas tree was put up. Inge felt that she had no right to enjoy it: would look at it on pain of whatever was the Jewish equivalent—she did not know

25

what it was—of hell-fire. If they had ceased to be Germans and could not become English, if they had to be Jews, then would it not be a good thing, she wondered, to be as Jewish as possible? She began to keep all the observances she knew of, attended all the religious services in the little hall; it was her way of hitting back at Dolph who seemed no longer to care what she was up to and would have no idea where she was; he had ceased to have time for her, was always surrounded by people and about to do something or other, or deep in a conversation that was private and could not wait. Even the staff consulted him on occasion, knew him by name. Everybody knew him: he had become an important person in the camp.

Rudi, who had seemed so capable of looking after himself, one day complained of a sore throat and the next was in the sick-bay with diphtheria, then still a killer. Inge prayed for his life, and wrote to him at such length and so often that her letters themselves were a declaration of love; she tried to keep her emotions out of them and let herself go instead about what was in her mind. Schools and adopters, she wrote, were on the look-out for talent: musical children and those who could paint were being given their chances, why not a child who could write? But how was she to prove that she would be able to write in English? Rudi wrote back, in pencil; the paper had buckled under his feverish hands. As soon as he had recovered enough to travel, his relations came and carried him off; he did not even manage to say good-bye.

"Those who play football with my heart," she wrote, "angels or devils . . ." Her abused emotions were behaving like drunkards; she had to have somebody and she still believed that only her brother was unique, irreplaceable. The gap left by Rudi she tried to plug with Werner; she was in his Hebrew class—she herself taught a class of beginners—and again and again, through the lessons, she caught his eyes resting on her budding titties, with what to her looked like disapproval; he had a stunningly austere face. "One cannot work through the heat of the day," he told them. "The word for before the dawn—" The hunchback Annie said, "It's in the Kinnereth song," and sang the phrase, in a voice that made the others hold their breath. "Sing all of it," Werner ordered her, staring at Inge's breasts.

26

But Inge had forgotten him; what shook her was not the beauty of the voice, nor that it belonged to Annie whom she had despised, but that one who owned such a talent should not have shown off with it. It was one of those minor accidents that mark one for life. Its effect was immediate: they were very short of material, in German, on Eretz Israel and she wrote a story for Annie to read out loud without letting anyone know that it was her own.

After the reading, Dolph said to her, "That book that story came out of, give it to me, there must be other things in it which we can use."

Werner detained her, after lessons, with talk of Judas Maccabeus and Bar Kochba: soldier Jews. She asked, "But how can we fight the Nazis?" and he said, "Not them, little sweetheart, but the English." He took her out of the rowdy hall into the sea-sodden night and with an arm about her shoulders said, "If that brother of yours had any spunk, he would rescue your parents." If he wanted to know how to do it, let him come and ask him.

Dolph—and Inge—had heard of *Aliyah Bet*, the illegal immigration into Palestine, everybody had heard of it. Werner claimed to have been given the task of recruiting likely youngsters—but before going any further, he told Dolph, Dolph would have to be sworn to secrecy. "We can't have you blabbing about it to your lover."

It mortified Dolph that he had been unable to see it for himself; that Rudi was a homosexual explained a number of things about him which had been baffling; Dolph felt cheated because he had believed that Rudi had valued him for his intellect. That Werner took him for another pervert did not bother him: he did not care about Werner. But he had made it his policy never to turn his back on information, and so he swore secrecy and confessed that two years before he had packed his rucksack and set out for Spain with the intention of joining the communists fighting against Franco. Werner laughed at him, "You're still a bit young, and you'll never be inconspicuous!" and advised him to equip himself with some indispensable advantage, for instance a knowledge of Turkish. Rather to Dolph's surprise, he was able to supply him with a Turkish grammar.

Every evening, over supper, the loud speaker gave out the names of those who would be leaving the next day; Inge was not listening but, as usual, day-dreaming when her name was read out; all she heard was "Stein". It needed her table companions to tell her that it was she who was meant: to be ready at seven o'clock in the morning to leave for a girls' boarding school. It was her worst nightmare come true: she could not, when she most needed him, find her brother; she had to go to the office on her own, to find out if she had even got it right, and could not bear the suddenness of it. "You've been here three weeks," they reminded her—three weeks? it seemed like much longer—"There are children in Germany waiting for your place." She was not certain what was meant by "boarding school"—always said in English; she could have asked, but did not believe that they would really know what the school was like, or, knowing, really tell her; it was in Manchester and she did not know where that was.

Her eyes streaming with tears which froze on her cheeks, she ran to her chalet, and then to her brother's chalet and then up and down the identical rows lit by lamps at the corners, where the washrooms were. Once she slipped on some ice and tore her stockings, she would have welcomed a worse hurt. While she was at the bottom of the field she saw the sea with its house-high waves—the night itself was weeping salt spray here; she would have drowned herself, she thought, if it had not been so cold. Back she ran, needing to pee but unwilling to shut herself into a lavatory for fear of missing her brother—by now also looking for her; they must have passed and re-passed each other with a chalet or a row of chalets between them. When she wet her knickers they froze to her skin.

They found each other not long before lights-out; he told her that she was wanted in the office and they were both in such a state that they needed strangers to explain between them that this was a second, later call: one of the girls on the list had a sister who had been left out; her reluctance to go had been noted; she could stay. They left the office holding hands and skipping, laughing, no longer feeling cold or homesick or cursed. All that had happened was that part of their birthright—to be together—had not been taken away from them, or not yet; to them it felt as if they had received a fantastic bonanza.

A few days later they had a letter—the first letter they had ever received with an English stamp: Rudi was proposing to visit them. He had chosen the day when the local cinema ran a matinee for the camp children—so that he could catch them on their own. Dolph could not have felt more threatened if Rudi had been a known killer. "They're showing a film I've always wanted to see," he said. In Germany, ever since they had been old enough, Jews were no longer allowed in the cinemas; but he could not tell her what film it was and Inge threw herself on him with such vehemence that they nearly fell over—believing that Dolph intended making himself scarce so that she could be alone with Rudi. Being refugees, they were both discovering, was turning them into liars; he did not even consider the possibility of enlightening her: could not cope with her emotions in addition to his own or rather, he told himself grimly, in addition to Rudi's. He slunk off in the midst of the camp crocodile feeling that he was the only hunter and leaving her, a gazelle, in lion-country—though the predator had no taste for gazelle but only for man; so pleased was he with this conceit that he marched away grinning.

With her head full of the beginning of a poem—watered-down Rilke—Inge waited out in the cold by the main gate; she would have gone further, for the sake of those extra minutes in Rudi's company, had she known from which direction he would be coming. She had not seen him since before his illness, almost did not recognize him in his new English tweeds, striding along as if he owned the road. She mistook it for love but it was only the reunion itself that made her heart turn over. They took hold of each other with all their hands, Rudi asking, "What's happened to David?" He was the first one to call Dolph, consistently, David.

She did not quite know how to tell him, blushed, fidgeted, while he warmed her cold hands between his which were colder in spite of his leather gloves. "He hasn't got diphtheria?" His concern made Inge blurt out where he was. "Then you and I shall entertain each other until he gets back," he said, and for warmth took her arm as they walked up to the hall. Having promised them entertainment, and nothing coming from her except demanding looks out of voracious eyes, he talked of

London: Piccadilly Circus, Buckingham Palace, Marble Arch—magical names. "I'll show you," he said in a heedless moment, his mind on David; she missed what he said for a while after that, her ears stoppered with emotion.

Dolph was not altogether surprised to find Rudi still there, waiting for him; he even caught himself being glad to see him: he had after all been his friend. But, shaking hands, he found, or believed that he found, his hand held a little longer than was conventional; he felt itchy all over under Rudi's scrutiny. Rudi said, "You've made other friends, and you want to get back to them . . . " and Dolph was reminded that what had been so nice about being with Rudi was that one did not have to explain oneself to him. He said something about having to see Werner.

He had expected Rudi to look at him like a girl; out of his knowing eyes at odds with his boy's face Rudi looked at him like a mother, and sighed and, looking away, said, "Perhaps I ought to have warned you about Werner, but, you know, one doesn't want to be over-protective."

Dolph was subject to sudden rages, and as a small boy could be made apoplectic by being called a turkey. In the days before Hitler, on their way to primary school, they used to pass a farm and you could get the turkeys to blow up their wattles by waving something red at them and challenging them to match it: Dolph enraged was the colour of inflated turkey-wattles. Inge, gazing at Rudi loving her brother—it seemed natural to her that everybody should love him—had not been listening and did not care what upset him: thought only that it was selfish of him to tell her to go away as if he knew nothing of her feelings for Rudi.

When they were rid of her, Dolph asked, "Is Werner another pansy?" Rudi turned away, and when he had got himself under control turned back and said, coldly, "My dear boy, he's something much worse, he's a revisionist. The worst thing about present British policy isn't that it is keeping you out of the Promised Land but that it is tempting Jews into terrorism. Some actions are too high a price to pay for survival, even one's own."

Dolph, wishing that they could go on with the discussion, was reminded that it was just as well that they no longer shared a hut, and demanded, "Why did you bother to come, you must know . . ." Rudi's face grew innocent with pleasure. "Of course

I know, dear boy, you have nothing to worry about!" and while Dolph was thinking, he sounds like a pansy, how could I ever not have known it? told him, "My relations have agreed to offer you both a home."

"*Scheisshund!*" Dolph said, and got away from him.

By the time Rudi decided to follow, he had disappeared in the crowd. You could hardly hear yourself speak in all that noise, let alone be heard if you called out to someone; Dolph could have evaded him for ever, in that press of people, but decided to come back because he had thought of saying, "What is really shitty is that you made use of my little sister—" and realized that it was himself who had made this possible. Rudi looked at him with more love than most young men have to offer, and said, "I didn't tell her, dear boy, that is why I waited for you." Since it would have made for an easier quarrel Dolph suspected a trick. Rudi explained, "You are the head of your family here in England."

Shrugging himself back down to size—the blood dismounting always left his eyes brighter—Dolph said, "You must know that it's out of the question."

"But why?" Rudi asked. "I can't help loving you, don't let it spoil your chances. Don't concern yourself with it, it's my problem not yours, you know me well enough to know that I shall never molest you."

Dolph thought, you are molesting me now, mentally.

Rudi said, "Think of Inge."

As if this could be made to serve him as a weapon, Dolph said, "My sister Inge is in love with you."

"Is she, dear boy?" Rudi asked, grinning: he was flattered. "Well, you know your Heine!" who wrote that everybody loves someone who loves someone else. After a time he said, "My relations will guarantee you both your education, and to people like that that means also university."

Later, Dolph learned to accept Rudi's love as a sort of compliment, the least self-seeking love he was ever to be offered; but just then all he wanted was to find something to say that would put an end to it. "If the choice lay between going to London with you and a concentration camp . . ." he began, and ended with telling him to go to hell.

31

"My dear boy," Rudi said, having heard him out, "I am there already."

Dolph was after all the one who would have deserved him: seeing that he had made himself clear he could afford to pause and imagine what it must feel like to be Rudi. "I'm sorry," he said, sincerely enough, and lied, "I didn't mean to hurt you."

It was Dolph being nice to him that was too much for Rudi. He fought his way out of the hall, that the cold night air might cure his stinging eyes or the dark hide his tears; he must have been aware of Dolph in his wake.

As he was walking rapidly towards the gate, Dolph caught up with him. It had occurred to him that if Rudi's relations were willing to help, perhaps they would help his parents. But it seemed to have become an impossible thing to ask. And for that, Dolph instead of blaming himself blamed Rudi.

TWO

JANUARY–JULY 1939

(The Sparrows)

MR AND MRS SPARROW had long lived with the idea of adopting a child; Rosie was in her early forties before she managed to produce a son. That Christmas, reading in their newspapers about the refugee children, they decided to make him, then six months old, the present of an older sister: one of school-leaving age, Rosie thought, who would be a help to her— and keep house for him after her death until he got married; Johnnie thought that she ought to be no more than ten, still young enough to become a real daughter.

As they walked among all those available children noisily eating their Sunday lunch, they were genteelly bickering, until their attention was caught by Inge, just then telling a story, looking a lot more vivacious than she was. They felt shy about approaching her, got one of the people waiting at the tables to find out her name, and, when they saw themselves being pointed out to her, hastily withdrew to the office to study her file.

When she was introduced to them, Inge thought that they would do: not realizing that she was practically orphaned, she was not looking for a couple to replace her parents; she wanted to keep at least her internal privacy and they looked self-satisfied enough perhaps to let her do that. They were both built on a large scale and there was something about the man that made her like him, perhaps no more than the way he did his hair: it was mousy, not pepper-and-salt, but it was combed straight back without a parting, like her father's. She welcomed the idea of having a baby in the family, too young to know that she wasn't a real sister, to whom she could be a Dolph, who would be unable to reject her because she didn't belong to him, would be as safe to love as a bear but more responsive; and a lightning conductor.

She talked with them, for five minutes or so, through an interpreter; it was agreed that they should go home to think about her and come back the following Sunday to take her out. They could not tell her what she most wished to know about them, which was what Dolph thought of them.

Ever since Rudi's visit he had been irritably rude to her; she did not know then that he was feeling guilty about having made a decision which concerned them both without consulting her, and thought, too late, that it would probably have been all right for her to have gone to London by herself. Feeling unfit to be responsible for her made him, temporarily, hate her; she was aware of it and, being Inge, blamed and hated herself. She dashed off just the same, and only within sight of him remembered and slowed down.

"Are they worse than anyone else would be?" he asked, sounding as if he did not care, when what he meant was that, in his opinion, she could not expect to find someone who deserved her. "I won't always be around to hold your hand," he said, with regret in his voice, and she believed that what he regretted was having had to do it for so long; she believed that he wanted to be rid of her and did not blame him. If she had been Dolph she would have wanted to be rid of her, too. She had the impression that instead of listening to her he was counting to twenty, because after letting her babble on he interrupted her in mid-word to ask, "Do you think that they would guarantee Mutti and Papa?"

It was with this thought in mind that the first thing many children wanted to know about their prospective adopters was what make of car they had. The Sparrows had come by train. Mr Sparrow was an accountant which, Dolph decided, told them little about his income. They lived in Buckinghamshire and this, with its royal connotation—Buckingham Palace—sounded upper-class to them. Inge had been told that she would have her own room. "What sort of house do you think . . ." Dolph asked, and she hung her head: he always managed to think of a question that spot-lit how inadequate she was; she could not bring herself to tell him that though she had seen it, in the background of the snapshot they had shown her of their baby, she had not taken it in: too busy thinking that if she had a son like that she would not let a Jew get anywhere near him.

34

She had noticed that Mr Sparrow's shoes needed heeling, she said, which made Dolph laugh at her: if he could not afford to take them to the mender's—and those two knew about having unmended shoes, even in winter—how would he be able to afford to feed another mouth—they knew also about going hungry. "Then what do you think they want me for?" Inge asked, aghast, and Dolph stopped smirking and even took her hand. In his new adult voice he said, "They've got to send you to school for at least another year, it's the law." A year! Inge thought, and did not dare to ask him how long he thought they would have to stay abroad: her mother had promised to look after her collection of toy animals until she got back. Instead, she began, "If I go there and I don't like it, Dolph . . ." He cleared his throat and said, "Some children don't like their own parents but they have to stay with them. We're luckier than most because we have a choice." But he stood shifty-eyed and was counting her fingers, as he tended to do when he was talking down to her.

Because he ended up by being so nice, she asked him to come as well when she went out with them: not an unreasonable suggestion in view of her lack of English; but he exclaimed, his face going mulish, "What makes you think I'm still willing to wipe your arse for you?" which made it impossible for her to ask him again.

He was not even about, the next Sunday, when the Sparrows carried her off. To make certain of not being tempted to snatch her back from the brink of her independence of him, he went into hiding to look out for their arrival: they came in a fairly new Rover. His employer had lent it to Mr Sparrow as his contribution to the refugee cause but Dolph did not know that then.

Inge had been afraid that she would not recognize them but—at Johnnie Sparrow's suggestion—they had come dressed the same: making Inge think that these were the only good clothes they had. She was allowed or made to sit in the front; she would have liked to look out at England but the man—wanting to share his enthusiasm with her—insisted on explaining the dashboard. "Yes, yes," she said fervently, the one word in ten which she understood being no help at all but wanting him to be satisfied with her. Already she felt that it would be better to continue with them than to have to start all over again with strangers.

They took her to a hotel. She believed that they were staying there and wondered if they would keep her with them overnight; no one had told her to bring pyjamas. Had her English been perfect she could not have asked them about it: in case they thought that she did not want to stay, or in case they thought that she did but was not meant to. She had never seen a public place furnished so richly and with such attention to detail; in Germany, no Jew had been allowed in such a place for as long as she had been old enough to have been taken there. So this is England, she thought, as if the camp were not England too.

They sat down at a table barely large enough for the plates (with doilies) of bread-and-butter and scones and the three-tiered cake stand, newly-filled, and the silver tea-pot and what she thought was a coffee-pot—it held hot water and she thanked God that she had not asked for coffee—and milk jug and sugar basin with silver tongs. She dutifully asked for milk in her tea and did not take the cake she most wanted in case one of them most wanted it too and left off eating before she was full, as her mother had taught her to do when she was visiting, and smiled whenever words or understanding failed her which was often, and wished by turns that it would look as if she did, and as if she didn't belong to them, and ceased to wish for her brother to be there with her because she would not have wished so much embarrassment even on a Nazi. The atmosphere was subdued, as if they were all Jews with no right to be there and afraid of provoking a pogrom. She looked round surreptitiously, not wanting the couple to think that she was more interested in the surroundings than in them, though this was true and she felt guilty about it, not realizing that it was because words literally failed her and for the surroundings her eyes were enough.

Dolph, watching the Rover carry his sister off, felt as if it were taking his innards away. If he had gone with her, he told himself, how could she have found out whether or not she could cope with those people on her own? But supposing they said or did something to upset her? Supposing there was an accident—and she was taken to some hospital, nobody knowing who she was or that she did not understand much English, they would think that her brain had been damaged and she would let them, because she always believed that other people were right . . . . *Liebe Mutti*, he started writing in his head, I had to let Inge out of my sight and a terrible thing has happened . . .

With an hour or more to kill before she got back, he strolled into the office. Since Rudi's visit, to reassure himself that his reactions were normal, he had been philandering; he did not think refugee girls fair game and made do with the students, which was also good for his English. He found it useful to pretend that he knew less than he did, which was easy because of his accent. For instance, the Cambridge student who had interviewed him and his sister was called Muriel, he pronounced it Mooriel; she tried to correct him until she concluded that he was doing it on purpose to tease her, but his ear was so bad that he could not even hear the difference. "He wants you to know that he thinks you're a cow," another girl told her. "He's quite the little bull, look at those bovine eyes!" Bovine, Dolph memorized, flashing them each a look that started them giggling. He had refused to take the intelligence test which Muriel had gone to the trouble of arranging for him—he had believed that it would commit him to the trade school; now that he knew better he felt that he owed her something. Gazing at her, he stroked the skin above his mouth, pretending that he was preening a moustache, and she told her friend, "That one thinks that he owns the world." He was amazed to hear it.

He thought, a dog's turd got up to look like the young Lord Byron—which was what the typist had told him he looked like. He felt more at ease with her, who was called Jean Crowther, because she was older—in her mid-forties—and was known to be Jewish which so many of the staff weren't. She, he thought, had recognized him for what he was when he had made a fool of himself, politely reminding her of the ribbon while she was typing a stencil. He offered to do something to help and she told him to draw a chair up, and gave him a pile of envelopes and a sheet of stamps.

He was half through when she said, "Don't blame yourself for not giving your sister more of your time. It will have prepared her a little for your separation." He had to stop breathing, and

37

swallow, before he could ask—meaning to pass it off lightly—"Do you always read people's thoughts?" He had meant to show her a casual face but his eyes were brimming. Her look of compassion went into him like a bullet.

He was still there, diligently sorting paper clips from rubber bands—a boy's equivalent of smoking a pipe, he supposed, kidding himself into believing that he had calmed down—when Inge got back; he had promised her that he would be there. To see him brought her as much relief as if the whole of her ordeal and not just the beginning of it were over; she pounced on him and led him up to her couple as if he were a trophy. He shook hands with them clicking his heels and bowing: to the natives this may have looked absurd or Prussian but it made Inge feel guilty for not having curtseyed when she greeted them.

Mr and Mrs Sparrow had decided to ask to be allowed to take her away at once: to them, the reception camp seemed a ghastly place for her to have to be in for another week; they feared that if they left again without her she would believe that they were still undecided and feel hurt; she pleased them and they were raring to look after her. Being English, they gave none of these reasons but, addressing themselves to Jean Crowther whom, because she was older, they believed to be in charge, they explained that that day they had been able to come by car but it was not their own . . .

What sense Dolph chiefly made out of their argument was that they were either too poor or too mean—and how big was England, how far could it be for them?—to come back for Inge; if she was worth so little to them, or if they were worth so little, Dolph thought, what did that augur for her future? On the spur of the moment—or that was what it felt like to him—he decided to accept, after all, Rudi's offer: he would see her settled and if he felt morally blackmailed by Rudi he would then get out. Jean Crowther had just given him her London address and told him that she would always be good for a bed and a few meals.

He said, to her, "We don't need these people." The student in charge of the office who had come over reminded him how long he and his sister had already been there, longer than most of the children. Dolph said, "I shall take her to London in the morning." Even to Inge, it sounded like no more than boyish fantasy.

The girl said something to the Sparrows, perhaps that allow-

38

ances had to be made for these children who had grown up under Hitler; what Inge thought she said was that children like her brother should have been left in Germany for Hitler to deal with. Knowing that whatever she said in German might not be understood and that to say what she wanted to say in English was beyond her, she screamed, wordlessly, clinging to her brother. To the Sparrows it must have looked as if she objected to being taken from him.

Her screams brought the camp commandant out of the inner office. The students, the typist, the would-be foster-parents all started talking at once. Dolph, rightly believing that he was the only one there who understood the situation, put his sister behind him and stepped forward and, making up in volume for what he lacked in diplomacy, shouted, "Listen to me!" The commandant, by-passing all the pitfalls of communication, took hold of him and propelled him into his sanctum, dispensing instructions over his shoulder and leaving the sister to follow.

He took no notice of her, who was at his mercy while he held her brother; lecturing him, he bullied him into the corner furthest from the door—and from Inge—and stood barring the way, barricading the children off from each other; Dolph could do nothing and Inge, being Inge, suffered what happened without doing anything.

They must have been allowed to say good-bye; in Inge's memory the camp commandant remained between them, as much of an obstacle as a railway station turnstile.

Bundled into the back of the Rover, she crouched shivering and silently crying, keeping her eyes shut so that she need not see for herself what it was that Dolph had discovered about the couple; his behaviour had convinced her that to be carried off by them was the worst thing that had ever happened to her. That he had not wanted to be separated from her even more than she had not wanted to be separated from him did not occur to her until years later.

Rudi said of her that she lacked a sense of proportion; she was to be adult, married, before she understood what he meant but it was true: she was equally upset about those of her belongings which had been unpacked and had been bundled back into her suitcase by some student; she felt like skimming that layer off and throwing it out of the window—would have done, she thought, if she had known how to open it—before it contaminated the contents underneath which had not been spoiled by the touch of alien hands. Johnnie Sparrow, a born father, had put the case not in the boot but at her feet because she had been so unwilling to let go of it.

The Sparrows must have had heart-heaving second thoughts about her. They told some of them to each other, their voices as smooth as the engine; she had heard about English conversational topics and from the sound of it they might as well have been talking about the weather. They meant to be reassuring, but she would have found it easier to think of them as people with whom she might one day come to feel at home if they had talked with passion and made use of their hands.

When Johnnie Sparrow could stand her misery no longer and stopped the car, she half-expected that they would throw her out: obviously the adoption wasn't working for either side; he went to the boot and when, from there, he came and opened the door on her, she half-expected to see some makeshift weapon in his hand. She flinched from him when he laid the rug about her; he offered her the use of his handkerchief and the thought of it made her retch; she understood it when his wife told him to take the blanket away: not knowing that it belonged to his boss, Inge believed that she was being judged not worthy of it, it was soft and a green-blue plaid. If they didn't hold it against her that she was a Jew—and she half-believed that they didn't—they must hold it against her that she was a refugee. So what, she thought, was the point of her having left home?

Under cover of the rug, as they drove on, she tried to undo the string from the broken handle of her suitcase, with the thought of using it to strangle herself; she could not get it off. She was surprised to have been asleep when she woke up, under street lamps, in the parked car, and was tempted to let the stranger carry her into the house, as he was about to do, as if he had been her father. Then she remembered her brother's berserk behaviour and, putting her feet down in Buckinghamshire, said, "Is okay." They rewarded her, and each other, with smiles.

Her one consolation all along had been the thought of Georgie but he was not there; she believed that they were telling

her either that he was not really their own or that they had
fetched her on behalf of Mrs Sparrow's sister. She was not even
sure that the house they were in belonged to them: during the
past week, they had begun to clear out and redecorate the small
room at the end of the landing, just big enough for a bed; they
were going back and forth undecidedly between that and the
back bedroom, where Georgie had so far been sleeping—Inge
was reassured to see his cot, and the parcels of baby things
waiting for him to grow into, including toys, which littered the
single bed.

It was the nicest room in the house and they wanted to give it
to Inge, but it had in it a wardrobe and a chest of drawers
crammed with their belongings for which there was no space
elsewhere, and they were wondering if she would not prefer the
smaller room which could be altogether her own. She gave up
trying to understand them and answered, alternatively, please
and thank you; all she wanted was to be allowed to curl up in
some corner and cry herself to sleep, but when they asked her if
she would like to be shown over the rest of the house it was the
turn of please, and so Mrs Sparrow did that. In the kitchen, she
showed her where everything was and Inge, believing that she
was being offered a choice of tea or coffee, and cornflakes with
tomato ketchup, began to shake her head and say, no, no, no.
Mr Sparrow, meanwhile, had cleared the bed and Inge helped
Mrs Sparrow to make it up with, for some reason, old sheets;
she was kept awake by the seam down the middle and by the hot
water bottle, and when she had cried herself as dry as the
camel-run desert in the Promised Land, she lay masturbating
thinking of her brother.

She awoke to the absence of the sound of the sea and to
sunshine, and to Mrs Sparrow bringing her a cup of tea.
Miraculously, her scant knowledge of English had been not
merely repaired but hatched somewhat in her sleep. As they
breakfasted together in the kitchen, they all three agreed that she
could not go on calling them Mr and Mrs Sparrow; they were
Mother and Dad to each other and when Inge—seeing them as
light-years away from her parents—volunteered to call them
that they got up and hugged her, from both sides. Mother
suggested that Inge was rather an outlandish name for everyday

use in suburbia but Dad said, "Inge is who she is," and for the first time she meant it when she smiled at him.

When Dad set out for his office, and Mother had kissed him good-bye, they encouraged Inge to kiss him good-bye, too. She resented their assumption that she must want to—and would have resented just as much being left out. Dad took hold of her by the upper arms, with one of his thumbs forward so that as she stood on tiptoe to reach him it touched the side of her left breast. She could still feel it there after he had disappeared round the corner.

Mother gave her one of her aprons to put on, but then took hers off saying, "Georgie, Georgie!" Inge wondered whether she was to be left, like Cinderella, to do the chores—and, when she wasn't, thought resentfully that she was not trusted to be left alone with all their belongings. Outside, she saw that she was now living in a semi-detached bay-fronted house, in a street—a neighbourhood—of such houses, told apart most easily by their front gardens: illustrating what Rudi had said, that the English conformed.

Because she had seen his photograph, Georgie looked familiar, forgetting that she had seen it, she felt, when she recognized him, as if there were an angel at her elbow. When he put his arms out to her, who was giving him her attention, instead of to his mother who was talking to her sister, she rashly opened to him all the chambers of her heart. "Go on, pick him up, love!" Mother encouraged her as if she knew of no reason why Inge should hold back. Perhaps because she was tentative about it, the six-months-old grabbed hold of her and clung. "O *du lieber Junge!*" she exclaimed, as if this fair northern boy were a reincarnation of Dolph. Into his ear went all the endearments she could think of, and invent, and other invented nonsense— and her thoughts spoken in German: him she would be able to tell things kept even from her brother.

After lunch—for which Dad did not come home—Georgie was left with a neighbour while they went to register her for school; that Mother was so willing to be separated from her own son for her sake reassured Inge more than words could have done. But she would have preferred to take him along—in the hope that people would mistake her for his sister.

42

As she used to think Dolph omniscient because he knew more than she did, she was over-impressed by Mother for knowing where to find a school which would have her; she had been prepared for any number of rejections first. Afterwards, they went to the shops where she was fitted out with a gym tunic and other clothes that translated her into an English schoolgirl. She dressed up as one when they got home to show Dad—and Georgie; it was as an English schoolgirl that she sat down that evening and sent her new address to her parents, to her brother, and to Rudi. His was the first reply, the first letter she received in her new home.

Dolph's first letter to her began, "Dear Jewish cuckoo in your English nest ..." tactlessly, or perhaps to remind her to remember who she was. But in the streets she was anonymous; the best part of each day for her was going to and from school, where they thought of her as a German. "Say something in German!" her school-mates said, and laughed at her when she did; they treated her as a half-wit because unless she knew what they were talking about she could not understand what was being said. Even in Germany—especially in Germany—among the members of the Hitler Youth, she would have been happy to stop being who she was to be like the others; she thought that in England she would be able to do it: believed that she was already half-way there by wearing school uniform.

It took days—weeks—before she could tell all the girls apart; to her, they were one as good as the other: all English. She started going about with the first girl who showed herself friendly, and when she became aware that she had put herself among the rejects she was pleased, as if she wanted the English to endorse what the Germans had thought of her—or perhaps to be made a victim of by her circumstances made her feel more at home.

Her friend kept rabbits and after her third, or it may have been her fourth day at school she went to see them; to be leaving school in another direction made her feel that life was beginning to open out for her; to be once again doing something that had not been arranged for her by others felt so right that she could not think of it as wrong: gave no thought at all to Rosie Sparrow watching for her with Georgie on her arm and slowly growing alarmed and then desperate—she could not even go out to look for the girl for fear that she would meanwhile arrive back at the empty house, locked out.

Inge, over-confident, lost her way; nothing was left of her spurious independence by the time she recognized, by the light of the street lamps, Johnnie Sparrow's pattern of rose-bushes. She was tired and hungry and ready to throw herself into her foster-mother's arms—had that one not greeted her scolding. It was the state Rosie Sparrow was in that made Inge realize, perhaps for the first time ever, her own value; but as a result she believed that she was bestowing her presence there as a favour.

There she was, coming out of the wet and cold dark like, she thought, a storm-tossed ship, and denied anchorage: the wrong harbour; it served her right for wanting to, wanting to cuddle and be cuddled by that large fair laced-up woman. Dolph and she had never been punished at home, God knows from where she got the idea that she must go up to her room without her tea, that was what she did. There was no key to her door; when her foster-mother knocked she waited, with her breath held and her hand raised—to hit out at her or to defend herself, she wasn't sure; but Rosie Sparrow trudged away again. When Dad came home Inge held her breath as much as she could, straining in vain to hear what the two of them said about her to each other; she wanted him to come up and give her a hiding—she had never had one—with her hairbrush or one of her slippers. She would have fought back and got hurt enough to make the committee take her away from them—Mrs Sparrow had told her, when she had questioned the outlay for her school uniform, that there was a committee which paid them to, ha-ha, look after her. But Johnnie Sparrow turned on the wireless.

By now she was sufficiently familiar with the household routine to know what they were doing; she found it hurtful to imagine it with her left out. Now she did not want to have her privacy respected, it did not feel to her as if that was what they were doing: more as if they did not care about her, as if they had forgotten that she was there. To distract herself, to make the evening pass, she started doing her homework, on the bed— there was no table, she would normally do it downstairs; It felt to her as if she were only pretending that there would be a tomorrow: it felt to her as if her life had come to a stop.

She pushed her school books aside and began to answer Rudi's letter but, concerned that he should think well of her, she could not let herself go; she could not let herself go writing to Dolph because it resulted in one long accusation and had he not fought like a panther against their separation? In the end she wrote to her parents, her mother really, blaming her for sending her away and pleading to be allowed to come back home. She wrote unthinkingly without stopping, and weeping so torren- tially that she could hardly see, accusing her mother of wanting to be rid of her until she had to admit to herself that if even a fraction of what she had written was true then what was the point of writing to her at all?

Rosie Sparrow, got out of bed by her son and seeing the light from Inge's room falling on to the garden, made her a cup of cocoa and left it outside her door, knocking to let her know that it was there. In the morning all three chose to behave as if nothing had happened, and if Inge could have loved them, she would have loved them for it. The letter to her parents she tore up and flushed down the lavatory.

Just when she was beginning to think that she had got the hang of being an English schoolgirl, she was rejected as one, expelled in mid-morning, for having lice in her hair; she had probably got them from the golden-voiced Annie who had used to borrow her brush and comb when she could not find her own. Inge was as scandalized by the discovery as her mother would have been, silently calling herself Jewish trash and worse things which others had called her before she had become, worst of all, a refugee. She did not see how she could, in her disgraceful state, return to the Sparrows, after all they had done for her; the only thing left for her was to run away and be a gipsy. She was loitering in the park, which was not really on her way home, when she saw the familiar pram and ran to greet Georgie, before allowing herself to realize that he would be attended by Mother.

Georgie clamoured for a cuddle and she would have got less satisfaction out of giving it to him, because that was normal, than she got out of refusing it, making of him a temporary Jew: rejected and maybe also with lice in his hair—which was scant and canary yellow. While Mother read the note with which she had been provided, she stood pulling faces at Georgie, pretending to show him what it looked like to be crying, until Mother said, "A big girl like you ought not to cry in public."

Apparently to the English having lice was nothing very terrible; the first chemist they called in on their way home was able to tell them what they needed to do about it, so nonchalantly that Mother decided to ignore his advice to cut Inge's hair. It occurred to Inge, not for the first time, that perhaps Mother did not love Georgie very much, because she made a joke of treating his head, too. She and Dad took the whole matter so lightly that at first Inge believed that she knew better when they maintained that, certainly, her school was expecting her back.

Throughout their married life, they had taken their annual holiday at Easter, to get the benefit of the out-of-season prices, and gone to the seaside. That year they stayed at home and spent the money on private English lessons for Inge. Dad busied himself making a sandpit for Georgie, and a goldfish pond for Inge; he had not asked her about it because it was meant to be a surprise and in later years she hoped that she had managed to conceal from him that she had not wanted it. Mother spent her time spring-cleaning the house; she took Inge shopping for curtains to replace the nursery ones that were in her bedroom; she chose a bold pattern in daring colours, quite out of keeping with the rest of the house—but she got it. Wanting to show herself grateful, she knitted a hat for Georgie. "Blue for a boy," Mother said; but Inge had chosen it because it was her brother's colour. After Mother had twice commented on the funny way she had of holding the needles, she finished it in the privacy of her room.

She had always believed that private lessons during school holidays were for dunces; she did not expect her foster-parents to know better but felt insulted that Miss Pym should think it necessary to take her on. "You need a grounding," Miss Pym told her, making Inge think that she meant to reduce her

46

metaphorically to bits. Rudi had already warned her that for a proper understanding of the English she would have to read all their books, and as "a prime example of the English character" sent her G. K. Chesterton's *The Man who was Thursday*. She was just as bewildered by Miss Pym's choice, *Pride and Prejudice*—misled by the old-fashioned usage of some key words, and by Miss Pym's pronouncement that "it might have been written yesterday". This made her believe that the English generally still talked and behaved and lived that way; she thought herself lucky indeed to have fallen among the Sparrows.

By the end of the holidays her English was good enough to make her look forward to school, and to tackling an essay; in Germany her essays had been read out in class even by Nazi teachers, and sometimes to other classes because they were so good; her need to be like everyone else was tortured and torn by her ambition to be outstanding. They were given twenty-four hours to think about the subject, "An Easter I shall not forget", and she lay awake half the night, imagining herself in first-century Jerusalem, someone who was there when Jesus rode in on his donkey; the bell had already gone before she started having second thoughts: the Christians around her might take it amiss if she wrote about their Jesus—it was still to be some time before it dawned on her that he too had been a Jew.

On the spur of the moment, she wrote about Daphne—the nearest she could get to her brother's name—who was shut up for the holidays by her foster-parents in a small room— Georgie's room but with bars at the window; Dad had been talking about fixing bars so that when he got bigger he would not fall out. Daphne was left with sufficient bread and water, which went mouldy and stale, and a bucket—like the prisoners in the Brown House—to piss and shit in—Inge spelled it peas and shite. One thing led her imagination to another. Daphne could have screamed for help: she must have had a secret from the neighbours; Inge could not think of one except her Jewishness, perhaps not altogether convincing since the setting was England; she decided, for greater effect, to leave the secret unspecified. By the time her foster-parents came back, Daphne was too weak to attract their attention and they forgot that they had ever had her . . . .

47

The essay caused a sensation in the staff room, where it was passed from hand to hand with headshaking and some moist eyes; especially those who did not teach Inge, and could not have told her apart in the playground, were disturbed on her behalf; her teachers, including Miss Pym, who knew her best, argued that she was a perfectly normal little girl—considering her circumstances—who had settled in remarkably well— considering her circumstances. The headmistress, feeling it beyond her to tackle Inge, sent for her foster-parents, who were gratified by this official recognition of their status. When she saw that they were ordinary, decent people, she had not the heart to show them the essay and confined herself to discussing Inge's progress in general terms: quite satisfactory—considering her circumstances. To come up with something she suggested that the girl should be encouraged to change her name: Jane was perhaps not unlike Inge, and a good old English name. "Plain Jane," Mother said on the way home and Dad said, "That's not my girl, why, she's pretty! To me she seems sort of dashing, more like a Jill." So Jill she became.

The essay was returned to her heavily marked in red ink, correcting her grammar and her spelling; the bucket line bore, in the margin, the comment, "we don't use such words." It made Inge laugh aloud: where did Miss Pym think she had got them from? It bore out what Rudi said, that the English were hypocrites.

He wrote to her on pale green, textured, slightly scented notepaper, using one side only, and she answered him promptly, at least partly so as to get the reverse on which to write the fair copies of her poems. Her mother had used to say to her, "How can you make poems in the language in which we are being cursed!" When she repeated this to Rudi, he wrote, "Surely you are not going to reject Goethe and all the rest because of the Nazis, that would be thinking exactly as they are doing." There had been a time when she had expected to write in Hebrew, in which, through synagogue services and her grandfather's prayers, she was at least emotionally at home. But she experimented happily in English—writing what was to poetry as noughts and crosses are to drawing—until she confided to Miss Pym who told her that nobody could write poems in a language to which they had not been born. It did not stop her, but made a shameful secret, a vice, of her writing, whether done in German or in English; for years she commuted between the two, at home in neither.

School had provided her with a pocket dictionary, which drove her frenzied until she learned how to spell: she once spent a whole evening unsuccessfully searching for the word "occur", too proud to ask Dad, who only read newspapers, or Mother to whom magazines were books. The desk dictionary which Rudi sent her was her life-line. In return, he expected her to write to him in English. He took it seriously when she asked such questions as, why does God permit the Nazis? rarely telling her what to think, but providing her with stepping-stones to reach her own opinions, guiding her gently. When he had nothing to say he copied for her passages from his reading, or jokes from *Punch*; he told her that they were a measure of the extent to which she understood the English: because once she did they would make her laugh—they didn't make him laugh, yet. His were the letters she looked forward to.

She found it increasingly difficult to write to her parents. It had never been possible to tell them the whole truth—about how cold it had been in Dovercourt, for instance, how crowded, how lost she (and Dolph?) had felt. Once she was on her own she began telling them lies: sometimes making things out to be better so that they would not worry about her, sometimes making them out to be worse so as to diminish the contrast between her own life and theirs—and was punished for lying to them with the suspicion that they were doing the same. The worst aspect of being separated was not feeling homesick, but lacking information. The photographs she had of them were turning into lies before her eyes: they would no longer be looking like that, after six months more of the Nazis and being without their children. She would rather not have heard from them at all than be misled by their letters, preferred not to think of them to thinking mistaken thoughts. It was usually her mother who wrote, her father adding his signature to show that he was not in a concentration camp or dead. She began to leave their letters unread, merely opening them to see that his signature was still there—and drawing solace from rejecting her mother for believing her fabrications.

Correspondence with Dolph she could no longer manage at all. By now, the older Dovercourt Zionists were settled in Whittingehame House, the stately home that had once been Lord Balfour's, of the Balfour Declaration; they were trying to create, in the hills of East Lothian, unimaginably, an enclave of the Promised Land. Their committee, finding more than a hundred bright middle-class youngsters on their hands, talked of establishing a Jewish Eton; they provided a headmaster who wore highland dress and spoke not a word of German; the boy who translated his first speech—a future Israeli diplomat— interspersed it with his own comments in broad Viennese, "This gormless twerp expects us to . . ." and the Scot was delighted to be so well received. They had nearly mutinied when they had been offered an issue of, incredibly, Nazi-brown work clothes; they had got navy blue ones instead. He looked like a chimney sweep, Dolph wrote, when he worked as a stoker, getting up before dawn to light the kitchen range; he smelled of diesel oil, he wrote another time, because he was driving a tractor. Inge could no longer imagine him. In one more year, he wrote, she would be old enough to join them; in one more year Georgie would be toddling and talking; she was not sure that she wanted to be a probationer in a kibbutz in which Dolph was the biggest *macher*—the kilted Scot, gone by now, had called him his head boy. He was kept so busy with work and lessons and communal affairs that he had to kiss and cuddle his girl on moonlit walks—the only way to get any privacy. She was also called Inge; it was the name, he wrote, that had first made him look at her twice; he referred to her as "black-eyed Inge"—making the other one feel that she was to be blamed for failing to inherit the colour of their father's eyes; she tried to make herself feel better by despising Dolph for not knowing that, in English, to talk about black eyes meant something else. When she pointed this out he answered that he was depending on her letters to improve his English—they were trying to outlaw German and speak only Hebrew—it was intended to be a compliment on her command of English but she thought he meant that if her English had not been better than his he would not have valued her letters to him at all.

He sent a snapshot of himself, looking idiotically happy with his arm around a titch of a girl looking up at him adoringly; Inge cut her away but then could not bear to see him so mutilated and tore the picture into uncountable bits. It was because she still had to thank him for sending it that she chose one evening, when Mother would have got a baby-sitter so that the three of them could go to the cinema, to stay at home, thinking that if she were alone in the house perhaps she would still be able to write to him.

But of course she was not alone. When some class-mates had met her pushing Georgie in his pram she had told them that this was the brother she had brought with her out of Germany; since she had told them nothing about Dolph—would not talk about him in broken English to strangers—they had believed her. She made a game of pretending to believe it herself, wanted him to grow up believing it, constantly told him about it; Mother said that he looked like her brother, in spite of the disparity in their colouring, when she held him—because of the way he clung. She had discovered that by pinching his dimpled bottom she could make him cling more tightly. "He must have been lying on his rattle," Mother said when she saw his bruises; Inge learned to pinch him more gently in his tenderer parts. She had fantasies that Mother had died giving birth to him and that Dad had fetched her from the reception camp to look after them both; sometimes she took Georgie into her bed at night, crooned German lullabies—the only ones she knew—and Hebrew pioneering songs to him, and fantasized that Dad—with Mother dead—came to do to her whatever men did to their women— she still had only the haziest notion of what that was.

When she went upstairs to see that Georgie was all right, he was snuffling in his sleep and this was excuse enough for her to pick him up. "Come and help me write to that stranger in Whittingehame," she whispered into his bright, sweet-smelling hair, knotting him to her with her use of German; she would get Dad to take a snapshot for Dolph of her holding Georgie. That thought allowed her to put off writing her letter; instead she began to bounce the scapegoat on her knees to *Hoppla, hoppla, Reiter* . . . until she could almost hear her mother saying, "Not so wildly or it will end in tears!" and it did: Georgie banged his head and after a stunned moment began to howl; to be able to comfort him was so sweet that she found herself looking at the clock to see if there were time, before Mother and Dad came back, to quieten him if she started him up again. In Dovercourt, talking with other children about the night the synagogues burned, she and Dolph had discovered that what had happened in their home town had been as nothing compared with what had happened to Jews elsewhere: the lousy (?) Annie had seen people clubbed to the ground and trampled on in their blood. Perhaps, Inge thought, stifling her impulse to make Georgie cry again, she was more of a German than she knew; perhaps having grown up under the Nazis had damaged her beyond salvation by England.

About three weeks later, at the beginning of July, she went one morning to take the milk in and found her brother sitting on the doorstep; he raised the half-drunk pint in his hand and said, "I have no money to pay for this, do you think they will mind?" His accent made her squirm.

It had been one of her nightmares that when they met again she would not recognize him, and he had changed by far more than six months: was bigger and brawnier. The bracing air of East Lothian had got under his skin. Hitch-hiking to her had taken him three days and most of three nights and it showed: he looked too stuffed full of young life, she thought, to look like a tramp, he looked like a gipsy urchin, grubby all over. Even his eyes looked smudged. He stood there grinning his Dolphish grin and she said, "Come in, come in!" also in English, but did not get out of his way; now she understood why Faust had been willing to give up his soul in exchange for keeping one moment.

The sounds, behind her, of Mother bringing Georgie downstairs, made her think of her life as a full cup, with Dolph as its handle: when he was not there it was of no use to her, but when he was there it was the rest that mattered. She blinked, to make sure that she hadn't imagined him, and as if there had been something in her eyes, so she could then see him more clearly; she thought of touching him and the thought got in her way; she turned her back on him and found the sight of the breakfast kitchen unexpected, and reassuring.

"Look who's here!" she said, as if Dolph arrived often.

52

Georgie clamoured for her and she took him over and turned to her brother with the thought not of showing him to Georgie but of showing Georgie to him: tasting her drink and taking the handle for granted. Georgie dropped his biscuit to clutch at her hair with messy hands and Dolph, appalled, warned her, "He's getting you dirty!" Joggling Georgie on her arm she told that one, "Hark who's talking!"

"It's our Inge's brother," Mother called out to Dad. It seems unlikely that she recognized him: she must have known it by her foster-daughter's face.

Dolph found crossing the doorstep harder than his long journey, but Inge was not aware of it; she tried to stop him from feeling a stranger there by flaunting before him how much she was at home. With a few ballet-like movements she laid another place, thinking nothing of kissing Georgie, now in his high-chair, in passing, as was her custom; Dolph, upset that she had been reduced to having to love strangers and embarrassed by himself, took his face to the kitchen sink. "Not here!" Inge hissed at him, suspecting nothing worse than kibbutz manners; but he stayed there, letting cold water run across his eyes until he could trust them, while she fetched a clean towel, not wanting his face to be dried by what had dried their hands.

He found it hard to speak, to answer Dad's harmless questions—also meant to put him at his ease; it was Mother who said, "Let the young man eat." Reminded of being almost sixteen, he squared his shoulders—until Inge turned to Georgie and addressed him, too, as young man, not meaning to hurt her brother but needing to defend herself against the realization that he no longer belonged to her, anyway.

More than she wanted to be together with him she wanted to leave him and go to school as on any other morning: could not cope with the emotions his sudden presence aroused; though she mistook the need to adjust her heart for a childish desire to show off to her class-mates by saying, "My brother is visiting me."

"I won't be much good until I've had a sleep," he told her, standing over her closely and playing with her hair. "Can I try out your bed, littlest of bears?" It made her catch hold of his fingers, and kiss them, and give them back to him, and having let go was tempted to throw herself into his arms. She believed that what had brought him had been his letters to her left unanswered, and if she had asked him that was what he would have said; it would have made her find the words and him the means to keep together and everything afterwards would have happened differently.

When she came back at lunch-time, with permission to stay away from school for the afternoon and the next couple of days, he was still sleeping. He had had a bath, his black mop had dampened her pillow; no doubt he had left the tub for her to clean—she was wrong, he had even hung up the towel he had used. His face in spite of its suntan looked vulnerable without the brightness of his eyes; he was worth ten Georgies to her, a hundred, a thousand, he was worth all the babies she would ever have. As she looked at him his lips opened to let out a small moist sigh and she decided not to waken him: he would anyway not get out of her presence what she got out of his; she sat down to watch him sleep, and to love him, and to be his sister.

When he opened his eyes he was at once wide awake, unlike her; he had disciplined himself to be like that. "Is this their house?" he asked and, disappointed as she had often been by what he was interested in, she told him sulkily that of course it was. "Do they own it outright?" he asked her, studying her face; she did not know. "Do they have valuable things?" he prompted. "Has she got jewellery? Do you know where he keeps his papers?" Horrified, dumbly, she fetched her money-box and offered him her saved pennies. "Oh, Inge!" he exclaimed, and hid his face under the bedclothes. Well, she inwardly quarrelled with him, you were talking like a thief.

When he could face bringing himself back to her, still upset—his voice needed oiling—he commanded, "Take those clothes off!" She looked down at her English-schoolgirl disguise and he said, "Put on something in which I can recognize you!" Not wanting to tell him that she had grown out of most of the things she had brought with her from home—as if it were her fault—she said, "You weren't wearing anything in which I could recognize you!" and he pushed the bedding down to present himself in his skin down to his sweet navel—which she had used to be allowed to clean for him, not all that long ago, when they had taken their bath together once a week because they could no longer afford much hot water. "It's all right for you," he was telling her, "I haven't changed."

His unfairness—itself belying his words—left her speechless. But she found an old jumper—too warm for the day—willing to accommodate her titties. The spare clothes Dolph had in his rucksack—white shirt and grey flannels in need of ironing—were no better than those he had worn on arrival, but clean. While he was dressing, he started prowling about, opening drawers and the wardrobe and exclaiming, "What bloody cheek!" at finding the alien belongings.

He turned to her and, about to put on his tie, said to himself, "I don't need that yet," and stuffed it into a pocket. The look he gave her felt to her as if he were fingering her heart. He explained, "I had hoped that they might be able to guarantee Mutti and Papa. There's no point in asking them, if they can't, I don't want to upset them for you. You're all right with them, aren't you? You're happy?" But she felt that she had never been more miserable in her life than at that moment when she realized that he was less concerned about her, his Gretel, than he was about their parents who had sent them away. Seeing her so bothered, he did not explain that all these weeks and months he had relied on Jean Crowther, who had lately written that with so many Jews in concentration camps, she could not find anyone willing to take an interest in his father who wasn't. Instead he asked her, "Do you have Rudi's address? Do you have his phone number?" Though in their letters to her they had neither mentioned the other, she had taken it for granted that they, best friends, corresponded. What was of importance to her at that moment was not that they didn't but that she hadn't known it: it made her think that this was her brother's Harwich and all the island he was lay beyond her surmising.

She judged her poems not by their quality but their date: the more recent they were the more they mattered to her; she found an early one and handed it to him for the sake of the information on the back. He pocketed it, after a glance, and she decided at once that it could not have been any good (he read it when she wasn't watching and believed that she had copied at least the opening lines from somewhere). He said, "Even Papa still had a

55

telephone," and for ever after she rated all accountancy as below what even a Jew can achieve.

Oh, she was proud of him. Walking along the street in his shadow she felt better about herself, a little because she knew where the nearest phone-booth was and he didn't, and more because his presence so thoroughly took her back into their childhood that it would not have surprised her to see a Nazi stone come flying at them; but chiefly she felt that a boy like him could not possibly have a sister who was of no value.

Watching him through the glass panels, using the phone, she thought him adult and in control while he was getting short shrift; only after he had been hung up on did he realize that he must have been taken for one of Rudi's faggots. He called Inge into the booth with him, gave her the receiver to hold and instead of explaining—they had always had an understanding that he could count on her cooperation in exchange for telling her what was in his mind—he at once began dialling again, and only the prospect of actually speaking to Rudi made her put up with it.

Rudi was not at home. Prompted by Dolph she found out that he had not said when he would be back; he always went to the swimming-bath after work and sometimes did not get back until late. Brother and sister looked at each other as they used to do after pressing their noses to shop-windows. Though they grudged the pennies they decided to call again: Dolph coached Inge into saying that she was Rudi's cousin. "People like that are bound to have cousins they haven't kept track of," he argued; the thought of such a wealth of relations was like a Christmas display. She had just come from Hamburg and was only passing through London and had urgent news for him. With her eyes held by her brother's eyes, she soldiered through the lies; it got her the phone number of his office.

"It's me, Inge!" she said, breathlessly, and had to explain whom she wanted and again said, "It's me, Inge!" only to be passed on again. Of course she recognized Rudi's voice when she heard it; agitated beyond speech, she handed the receiver to her brother.

They arranged to meet at lunch-time the next day. The pioneers in Whittingehame had pooled their hearsay knowledge of tourist London and provided their David with a list; they went in on the train after breakfast but, enchanted by the stone lions and tame pigeons in Trafalgar Square, and by the mere thought of being loose in London, they got no further until it was time to walk up the Charing Cross Road to Oxford Street. Rudi passed right by them, they did not recognize him in his bowler hat and dark pin-stripe suit; he pretended to be meeting them by accident, a heart-easing joke.

But when he offered his hand to Dolph, that one put both his hands behind his back, saying, "You know perfectly well that people here don't do that." Inge could have kicked him: what bloody cheek of him, with his reckless English, to tell the gentlemanly Rudi how to behave! Rudi's face turned pink and Dolph's turned a darker shade. Rudi put Inge between them to take them to where, he said, they would be able to get real German food; he explained that he had joined the family firm with the intention of becoming rich and independent as quickly as possible. Dolph moved round to his other side and, interrupting him, said, "I'm sorry, that wasn't premeditated, will you shake hands with me now?" They did so and Rudi said, "It's all right, dear boy." Dolph, going the colour of turkey-wattles, exclaimed, "Can't you stop sounding like a pansy?"

"I'll try, dear boy," Rudi said.

Inge, who liked the flower for its romantic-sounding name—"little stepmother" in German—assumed that Dolph meant sounding velvety, suave; she believed that the cause of his bad temper was Rudi's oh so successful effort at assimilation: a cardinal sin in the eyes of all Zionists, who believe that not the Jew's difference but his endeavour to pass is what arouses anti-Semitism. She was thinking about this and did not notice that they had lost Dolph, several shop-windows back, until Rudi drew her attention to it, asking, "Shall we see what he finds so interesting?" To make up for her brother's rudeness, she took his hand; it was trembling and she believed that it was trembling for her. He returned the pressure she gave it and then let go; by this time they were back with David.

To the display of radios and gadgets, Dolph said, "I want to get it over with but I don't know how to begin," and for the next

57

few minutes the two young men debated whether or not it was all right for him to ask a favour of Rudi, Rudi maintaining that it would be a kindness to him, and that whatever it was David wanted, if it were within Rudi's powers then he should have it. Inge, hungry and looking forward to the German food, and annoyed with her brother for wasting so much of what little time they had together with Rudi on twaddle, finally lost patience and interrupted with, "It's about Mutti and Papa." Dolph shot her a glance of amazing gratitude, and told Rudi what he needed to know about them.

But then he said, "I can't let you buy me a meal and I haven't any money," it was too much even for Rudi; he walked off. Inge, loving them both more than providence should have allowed, was torn between leaving her brother without knowing where and when they were to meet again, and losing Rudi in the lunch-time crowd; to her shame and satisfaction she chose Rudi—arguing with herself that it was in the nature of things that brother and sister should find each other again.

She caught Rudi up and took his hand, and asked him why it was icy. "Because I have a warm heart," he said; she believed that he meant that it was warm towards her—which it was, though it was seething for another. But she let go when he pointed out that it wasn't done to hold hands in an English street.

Dolph caught them up as they turned into Charlotte Street; he must have stalked them: he was not even out of breath. He clapped a hand on Rudi's shoulder and said, "If you can carry it off, so can I, am I a worse man than you are?"

They had bratwurst and sauerkraut and other such things which stilled more than their physical hunger. The boys drank German beer—too much of it, Inge thought because they were in such high spirits: Dolph because he had overcome himself and Rudi because he loved him.

Afterwards, Rudi insisted on going to buy them presents, mementos of their encounter; he showed them the money in his wallet and they believed that he was already rich. He took them to Foyle's and bought Inge *The Oxford Book of English Verse*; for Dolph he bought the collected poems of Heine; to these destitute youngsters they were magnificent gifts. When Dolph demurred, Rudi told him, "I'm only buying it for you so that you can send me the little volume for which you risked your life, it's just the right size for taking with one into the trenches."

That was what brought it home to Inge that there would be a war.

THREE

AUGUST 1939–JULY 1940

(Miss Pym)

FOR THE REST of his life, Dolph did not forgive himself for not having asked the help of Rudi's relations sooner; when it became apparent that his parents would not be able to get out of Germany in time, he tried to unburden himself to one of the youth leaders whom they had on the training farm.

Would his parents' lives not have been worth a little, even homosexual, prostitution? Otto asked him as they walked up and down the corridor of the stately house for what privacy that would give them, since they could not go outside because it was raining. It would not even have amounted to that, Dolph explained miserably. Otto asked him to examine his reactions: why had he rejected Rudi's advances—he hadn't really made any—with such vehemence? He was not one who granted intimacy easily, yet with Rudi he had at once become friends .... Dolph suggested that it had had something to do with when they had met: just after he had left his home and everything familiar: Rudi had been the first stranger to take an interest in him. Had he perhaps encouraged his sister—"I didn't do that!" Dolph protested—so that he could be made love to by Rudi vicariously? Did he not identify with her to some extent? Everybody, Otto told him, putting a fatherly hand on his shoulder, was a latent homosexual, especially at Dolph's age.

His guilt feelings still unshed, Dolph now needed to unburden himself also of this conversation. The proper person for him to have turned to would have been Rudi, who would have understood him without too many words, and probably have found the right things to say to make him feel better; but Rudi had become taboo. The only friend available to him, Dolph felt, was his sister, who now received the longest most miserable and most baffling letter she had ever had from him. He accused himself of extreme selfishness, of intellectual dishonesty—she had no idea what this meant—and said that he could not bear to live with himself any more: he had broken one of the Ten Commandments—he did not tell her that it was the fifth—and would give his life to undo what he had done—she wept at the phrase without understanding that he meant it. Now he told her that he had tried, in Dovercourt, to have himself recruited for illegal rescue work. He had heard that if war broke out there would be a need for refugees who did not look Jewish—that was him—to act as agents provocateurs in German communities in London and other cities, to ferret out potential fifth columnists; he had put his name forward and was telling her about it so that if he were caught she at least would know with certainty which side he was on. She was to tell nobody—and that meant not Rudi either—and to burn his letter as soon as she had finished reading it. He would be issued with a false identity and in that case it would be better if she burned all his letters, and whatever photographs she had of him, and, not to endanger each other, they would have to break off all communication.

It had not occurred to him that she would feel the need to unburden herself, too.

She went down to the post office, with Dad to help her put a call through to Scotland; she would not have thought of it if Dolph had not telephoned Rudi. She spoke to someone in the office who told her that her brother might be anywhere on the farm and it would take far too long to summon him to the phone—though in fact he was next door in the library, polishing the floor. Would she like to leave a message? "Tell him I got his letter!" she shouted, desperately, and, more concerned with reassuring him than herself, "Tell him I understand it." Afterwards Dad suggested that she ought to have told them that she would ring again at the same time tomorrow, and Dolph could have been there, waiting—and out poured the tears which she had been struggling against because for a big girl like her to cry in the street wasn't done; it mortified her to realize that she had merely added to her brother's worries by ringing him up as if something were urgently wrong.

In the weeks before her fourteenth birthday, when Inge was

on holiday while Dad had to go to the office, Mother kept arranging treats for her: a visit to the London Zoo, to Kew Gardens, to Madame Tussaud's—for which Georgie was still too little. "Never mind," Inge tried to console him when he had to be taken out, howling, before she had seen everything. "We'll take you again in a few years' time and you'll enjoy it." Mother, overhearing her, said, "Oh love, don't live so much in the future, get what you can out of the present."—"But it'll be much nicer when he is old enough to be proper company for me," Inge argued, and wondered if what she was doing was what her brother had once accused her of: wishing away the most blissful time of her life.

Because the present really wasn't bad. She had only to say that she wanted something and, provided it didn't cost too much, she could have it: she got a season-ticket to the nearest swimming-pool, and a tennis-racket though it was second-hand. She only had to stop in front of a sweet-shop for Mother to fish in her purse for a coin to slip into her pocket.

They managed less happily when they looked over her clothes. She could not bear to discard the least scrap of anything she had brought with her from home. "But what is the good of keeping what you'll never be able to wear again?" Mother asked her and unwilling, or perhaps unable, to explain, Inge spread the skirt of a gingham dress and pointed out that there was enough material in it for a blouse—perhaps she could try her hand at making one? They bought a pattern the next time they went to the shops; but then she made excuses when the truth was that she could not bring herself to cut the dress up. "Well, you could wear that nice straw hat," Mother said and Inge exclaimed, scandalized, "That's for going to Palestine with!" as if it were a sort of magic carpet. They must have talked it over behind her back; Mother told her to pack whatever she liked in her old suitcase—its handle still makeshift with string—and they would buy her a new one to hold the rest of her things. "A suitcase?" Inge asked, made breathless by her imagination running hither and thither. "But where are we going?"

Mr and Mrs Sparrow had decided, because of the threat of bombing if war broke out, that Mother should take the children to her brother's in the West Country; when they had made enquiries about schooling for Inge they had been told that this was an area where she, with her German passport, would not be allowed to go.

They shirked telling it to her and she, having got used to expecting nothing except good from them, was mirthfully waiting for them to spring their greatest of all surprises on her birthday, when they in their perplexity had even forgotten what the day was until the post brought her a parcel from Rudi: a copy of *Jane Eyre*—which she had not yet read—and ten shillings "to spend on something girlish."

"You tell her!" Mother wailed to Dad, and hurried upstairs, weeping.

That Mother took it so hard put Inge on the defensive: did they think that after having had to leave her Mutti and Papa and being separated from her brother she would mind losing them, who less than a year ago as far as she was concerned had not even existed? Who did they think they were that they expected her to grieve for them? Now she saw everything they had done for her as a bribe to make her love them as if she had been their daughter—when their flesh-and-blood son loved them no better than he did her, a mere cuckoo to be got rid of again at the first opportunity. Did they think that she had been desperate, or stupid, or young enough ever to have believed that they were going to provide her with a permanent home: do more for her than her own parents had done? She was willing to believe them when they said that they would miss her, she hoped that they would, she hoped that they would die of remorse at having got rid of her. As far as she was concerned, they had not been her idea and she did not need them.

She did not need Georgie: did she not have Dolph?

Rudi wrote, "Pretending that you were their daughter was not the least but the most they could do. They could not treat you as a real daughter because in that case you could either have gone to the uncle's farm or stayed at home—" where Mr Sparrow remained, to go to work. But she was being passed on, third-hand, to her English teacher, Miss Pym. Instead of crying herself to sleep over it, Inge could not leave off reading *Jane Eyre* and blessed her for coming to her just when she needed her most, and decided that in future she would love only people in books, who could not fail her. Miss Pym's flat was so full of books that Inge looked in vain for where she would sleep—until Miss Pym undid an armchair in her study to demonstrate that it would turn into a bed, as if she had read her thoughts, making Inge believe, in spite of some of her comments on some of her essays, that they understood each other.

The outbreak of the war was marked for her by the first letter she got at her new address, again from Rudi: he wrote that Hitler was not the only one who believed that the English were unprepared and would be unable to stand up to him; one of his uncles had committed suicide so as not to fall into Nazi hands, another was emigrating to the United States. This was his favourite uncle and he had hoped to go with him but the family had vetoed it. Inge felt guiltily glad and looked up "veto" in his dictionary; it did not help her to understand what was behind it. He had enclosed a ten shilling note, because he wanted her to have her photograph taken—the rest of the money she should spend on Penguin books; he recommended some titles. Would she be so sweet, he wrote, as to sign it before sending it to him, "for all to see, as film stars do for their fans"; he suggested, "To Rudi with love from Inge". Not knowing that he needed it as camouflage against his persecutors, it sent her imagination on a marathon run. She wrote, "with undying love", dying being just then too much on her mind.

When school recommenced, late and chaotically, new slogans appeared on the lavatory walls. "The only good German is a dead German", one read, to which another hand had added, "That means you know who". Somebody had put, "Yids are yellow". That one baffled her: Georgie was yellow, she was almost black. "Why did they write that?" she asked the girl who kept rabbits, and was glad to add it to her collection of idioms: using them made her feel that she had the freedom of the language. When "Jews go home" got written up, she tried to explain that they would have liked nothing better, and it wasn't the Germans who were preventing them but the English, with their pro-Arab policies. Those who heard her, spread the word: the little German had come out against the English. At break-time she found herself cornered in the playground; just as it used to be in Germany, she thought. What was she going to do to help the Germans win? they asked her, and were not interested in having her position explained to them. Which side had her father fought on in the last war? "If the Nazis got hold of him and your mother," one said, "by threatening to do things to them, couldn't they make you spy for Germany?" She wished herself back there, among girls who merely pulled her hair and pinched her breasts; thirty years later that conversation was still giving her nightmares. If her brother fought for England and was caught by the Germans he would be shot as a traitor, because he was a German—however much she might make them all late for the next lesson by insisting that he wasn't.

"Daphne knew that her brother wasn't yellow," she wrote in her essay; Miss Pym made her leave it and go to get an aspirin, assuming that if she would not say why she was crying it must be because she was having menstrual pains.

Living with Miss Pym was like being permanently in class.

She said, "You are a guest and a guest has no duties except one, which is to make herself agreeable—" making a moral issue of passing the marmalade or emptying the pedal-bin. "Be agreeable!" she got into the habit of saying, until she was saying it whenever she saw Inge, probably without even being aware of it; in class she was always saying, "Sit up straight," to nobody in particular, mechanically. The first time Inge, anxious to be agreeable, asked if she should put some coal on the fire, Miss Pym said, "This is now your home as much as mine—" which was untrue—"which means that you can do as you please—" also untrue—"but please remember that it was my home before it was yours and will still be my home after you have gone." Becoming aware of Inge's stillness, she looked up and found it necessary to say, "Don't gawp, girl, it makes you look quite stupid—" which was how Inge felt. "Is it not true that you will grow older? Old enough to leave school and perhaps go to work in Fleet Street?" It outweighed a lot, her sympathetic awareness of Inge's ambition.

What made up for the fact that the only place of her own which she had in the flat existed only at night, was that she lay among books, like a cat let loose in a dairy; she was allowed to take out any book she wished, provided she put it back in the condition in which she had found it, and into the same space, and did not take out more than one at a time—even when she was choosing. "If it's too much trouble to put back and perhaps take out again," Miss Pym said, "it'll be too much trouble to read. The true book-lover likes to handle books."—"Oh, I like to handle them!" Inge assured her, and took on the task of keeping them free from dust.

Above the bookshelves were etchings of martyred men and women earning sainthood; the greatest of them, carved in ivory, hung on his olive-wood cross more permanently than Inge could close her eyes. He hung where she could see him from her unfaithful bed by the light coming through the glass-panels from the kitchen, where Miss Pym sat marking exercise books—exiled just like Inge, she liked to say, even in her own home. Inge, kept awake by the smell compounded of books and old furniture, and by her brother's hankering after spectacular adventure, pretended to be asleep when Miss Pym looked in on her. She did it nightly: and came forward to kneel over Inge; of course Inge knew what she was doing, try as she might to pretend to them both that she didn't; Miss Pym, getting into the habit, one night let fervour make her audible. "Sweet Jesus," she prayed, "have mercy on this miserable Jew." It left Inge breathless, buried under Christian compassion.

Dad had told her to look in on him at any time. When she had got over sulking for being considered too, as Rudi put it, nubile to be allowed to live alone with him, one day after school she set off in the old, the opposite direction, took the spare key from the garden shed—kept there under an upturned flower-pot ever since Mother had had her handbag stolen—and went in to get Dad his tea. As she danced between larder and cooker and table—singing, in Hebrew, of ploughing the desert and making it bloom, with a, she could feel it, Dolphish grin on her face at the surprise Dad was going to get when he came in—it was as if this were home and only Miss Pym were exile.

She had put the potatoes and the cabbage on to boil, to have with a bit of cold meat, and was thinking of making her special continental sauce before it occurred to her that perhaps now Dad's habits were not as dependable as they used to be; she was right: he did not come in until long after the vegetables were spoiled, and then not on his own but with another man of about the same age; they had been to a pub and already eaten and Inge, getting a hug from Dad—her first beery kiss—wondered how she came to be so familiarly in the arms of this stranger. For the next ten months or so, she avoided that neighbourhood for fear of encountering Dad and having to forfeit a kiss for once having been his pretend-daughter.

The Sparrows had never really got used to calling her Jill, but now there was nobody in her daily life who called her Inge; she wrote to Rudi, was it not dishonest, rather like Heine having himself baptised for convenience, or like people joining the Nazi party for the sake of keeping their jobs? This time Rudi failed her. He wrote that she was making a mountain out of a molehill (another item for her collection); that she had no sense of proportion. Had she no imagination either? (At other times he had told her that she had too much.) Europe was dying, the world was dying—and she was worried about her *name*? What did it matter what anyone called her: it mattered only that she should know who she was. Boys hardly out of school were going to lay down their lives (image of elephants trampling Jews to death in Egypt more than two thousand years ago). The letter went on for five pages, the exquisite handwriting deteriorating throughout; again and again he returned to the attack: rather than feeling sorry for herself (she had not known that she did; had not known that she did and it showed) she should concentrate on writing sustaining letters to him and to her brother (he put them in that order). If she meant to become a writer, she must cultivate an all-embracing compassion.

He did not tell her that her brother had written to him, demanding that, in the event of his death, Rudi should act as her guardian. "In that case it won't matter that you can't love her in the usual way," he wrote to him, "all that is required of you is that you should respond to her affection for you—of which she has far too much."

It was not affection she felt for Rudi just then; he had a talent for making people loathe him. His next letter followed too soon for her; she dreaded to open it but it was in fact a humble apology for his crudeness, his crassness—or whatever she

67

wished to call his shameful failure in friendship: the truth was that he had written just after parting in anger from someone who might well get himself killed in his monstrous flying machine—and he had been his best friend. The only grudge against Rudi this left her with was that he had a better friend than her brother.

She had been out to post her answer to this letter, and was still choosing herself a book to settle down with for the evening, when there was a ring at the door; it was a policeman. He was unwilling to believe that she knew her own name, until Miss Pym came from the study—she wasn't exiled except at night—and backed her up.

He had to be allowed in because the blackout demanded the shutting of the front door. Getting his notebook out he said, to Miss Pym, "She looks too young to be mixed up in this," and then read out, as if it were distasteful to him, Rudi's name.

"Yes, I know him," Inge answered, proud as much of its long standing as of her friendship with Rudi; she knew better than to fear an English policeman as if he were the Gestapo. "Yes, we write to each other." She was as unperturbed as if it had been the postman. "Just testing if you're telling the truth," the policeman said, with a glance at Miss Pym which made Inge feel outnumbered, and made her wonder what reason there might be for not telling the truth, in England, while the policeman was telling her that letters from her had been found in Rudi's room when it was searched. It stupefied her: they searched houses in *England*? It was not until afterwards that she felt gratified that he should have kept her letters, and wondered if they could possibly mean as much to him as his meant to her—she being only Inge—and tried to remember what she had said in them that had been read by strangers—*wildfremde*: there is no equivalent word for it in English, perhaps the English never feel wildly estranged.

Much later she learned what had happened. Wanting to make up their quarrel, Rudi had followed his airman to his base and unable to get into it, had put up in a neighbouring village where his enquiries about the off-duty hours and social habits of the local airmen—and his continental good manners which were more noticeable than his German accent—had aroused suspicion. The police had taken him in for questioning and had contacted his relations to confirm his identity and they, believing that it was a matter of his homosexuality, had abstained from standing up for him. Thus encouraged in their suspicion, the police had searched his belongings and finding that he had a girlfriend, had sent a local bobby along to question her. Asked if she knew anything about his politics, Inge exclaimed, "He has more reason to hate the Nazis than you have!" getting herself into trouble with Miss Pym without being of use to Rudi. On the principle then popular of better safe than sorry, he was interned.

Her brother was also interned, on Whit Sunday; she did not know about it until mid-June, when she received a letter written in a bold scrawl and signed Hansi. The community had been summoned to a roll-call in mid-morning, in the presence of the local police, who had read out a list of names. It had made no sense to the hearers: they had not been able to see what those who were on it had in common that distinguished them from the other older boys: it was their German passports. She had packed for David, Hansi wrote, so that he could spend his last moments talking to people; he had left a bucketful of broken hearts and chaos—Inge assumed that this was what people meant by poetic licence: the chaos must have been caused by the fact that the only older boys left were those who happened to have Czech or Polish nationality or were stateless. She had promised David, Hansi wrote, to write to Inge, who must understand that she was not his girlfriend—just the one he came to when he needed to talk; the females in his life were like rags in a broken window-pane—Inge wondered if Hansi put it like that because Dolph had told her that she wrote poetry—as he tried in vain to make up for the loss of his mother and his sister . . . . It stunned Inge to read this, she had always believed that their relationship existed entirely for her benefit: that Dolph put everything into it, put up with it, and got nothing in return. Yet at the same time she resented that she was a rag when she might have been a whole pane: that Dolph would have to give his babies to other females was something she could accept: but it was not taboo to make use of your sister for everything else. Poor little David . . . Hansi wrote, and Inge would have resented this even had she known then that Hansi was a year older and an inch taller; but

69

she, too, pitied him—without knowing how much reason she had for doing so.

Something or other had detained her in the classroom, one day after school, when a couple of girls came to tell her that there was a soldier waiting for her outside the gates; she thought that it was intended as a joke—Dolph was not yet seventeen—but it was Rudi; she had to look twice before she recognized him. He had been interned with other German nationals, some of whom were true Nazis, who took their frustration out on the effeminate Jew; he was one day to tell her that there had been times when he had thought that he would have been better off in Dachau. He seemed almost middle-aged: his hair still so short that it stood on end, puce pouches under his haunted eyes, and on his left cheek the scar of a cigarette burn which took some getting used to. He told her that he had other scars, which she would see if she ever saw him undressed; he meant, if they went to the swimming-bath together but she blushed and for a long time founded her dreams on this bit of misunderstanding. His relations, to help him live down his contretemps with the police, had pulled strings to get him into uniform as quickly as possible; he was not yet really fit but he did not tell her this. To his relations, being a private in the Pioneer Corps—no German national could be much more in the British Forces at that time—was also shameful; he had sought out David's sister because he urgently needed to see someone looking at him with shining eyes.

He had brought her news of her brother: they had had the good fortune to pass through the same camp at the same time; they had even managed to get beds next to each other, as in the reception camp. He was fine, Rudi said, David always, like a cat—a black panther, say—fell on his feet; as he began to speak of him, Inge caught sight again of the old Rudi. He said something about David having forgiven him; she thought he meant, for not managing to get their parents out of Germany in time. "Tell me what I must do to get him released," she pleaded. "Will you help me?"—"Certainly not," Rudi answered without hesitation. "He's much better off where he is, where he can't get into mischief." She asked him what he meant and he said, "Your brother, my dear Jill, is of the stuff heroes are made of." She thought that it was the nicest thing anybody had ever said to her.

She considered taking him home to tea: he was the most agreeable person she had ever come across and she would have liked to give Miss Pym the treat of his company; but she did not want him to know that she slept under a crucifix. That it would have provided him with the feeling—the illusion—of belonging (he could at least have felt that he belonged with her) after which he, too, must have been hankering, did not occur to her. To her, a cup of tea in a public place was as good as a feast.

Afterwards, playing at being a soldier going off to the war, he let her come to the station with him, and there he encouraged her to kiss him; for her it was the first proper kiss—proper also in the sense of chaste; it was the first time he had invited a kiss from a girl and he did not mind it nearly as much as he had expected.

He gave her a lot of chocolate: some of it was his ration which he had saved up, more had been given to him by the men in his unit when they had heard that he was going to visit somebody's little sister. When she got in, she showed it to Miss Pym so that she could take her pick. "I'll be no party to black market dealings!" Miss Pym exclaimed, snatching her hands away. "You people always exploit other people's misfortunes! It's an abuse of our hospitality." It reminded Inge to get out her commonplace book, to note what Rudi had said, that to the English nothing alien was human; it sounded to her like something said by Oscar Wilde, whom he was constantly quoting.

Inge wondered what sort of hospitality it was that took boys not yet out of their teens, who had sought refuge and had surely suffered enough from discrimination, took them from the safe anonymity of London, the safe remoteness of Scotland, just when they were beginning to feel at home, and concentrated them on a disused race-course in Surrey, right in the path of the Nazi invasion, to be handed over to them as a sop, Inge thought, or to be bargained away as Czechoslovakia had been? To take the sensitive, intellectual, city-bred Rudi, who had never in his life held a broom let alone a spade, and put him into a labour-battalion—was that not exploiting his misfortune? They were living under canvas like boy scouts, he wrote; he was to feel less cheerful about it in the winter mud and cold.

He had told her that the English intended sending the unwanted refugees abroad: David might spend the war trapping furs in Canada or farming sheep in Australia—Rudi thought that it would be a good thing for him, he was hoping for it. Then, late one afternoon at the beginning of July he sent her a telegram, asking, *Did David sail on the Arandora Star?* It was the first telegram she had ever received; she opened it with trembling hands covered in earth: she was helping Miss Pym to prick out some lettuces. "How do I know?" she wailed, and fled into weeping; she could not see why it should matter telegram-much to Rudi. Miss Pym took the form from her, read it, asked, "Who is David?" sniffed—she was allowed to do this though Jill wasn't, because Jill was not yet a judge of when it was out of place—and said, "Disraeli was just the same, so extreme about everything." It was to amuse Rudi one day, to have been likened to Disraeli; it would not have amused him then: the *Arandora Star* had been torpedoed off the west coast of Ireland with the loss of fifteen hundred lives.

The first letter Dolph had written to her from internment in Lingfield, twenty-four lines on a shiny chalk-white form, was not to reach her for another five weeks; the first letter she received from him came from Douglas on the Isle of Man and was worse than the one he had written when war broke out. His name had been down for the *Arandora Star*, but he had got another boy to take his place. "His name was Joachim Meyer," he wrote, "remember it! If, *Scheisshund* that I am, I ever do anything with my shitty life, it will be done in his memory." He had paid Joachim Meyer the twelve pounds which Rudi had left him—which was the money which Rudi had had on him when he had been arrested, returned to him on his release, less his fare back to London—and the wrist-watch, Dolph wrote, which Jean Crowther had sent him for his sixteenth birthday. Inge wondered who Jean Crowther was that she should have made him such a princely present.

She had a letter from her not much later, reminding her that she had worked as a typist in Dovercourt and explaining that she was writing to enlist her help to make her brother see reason: he would listen to *her* who was the most important person in his life—and again, it stunned Inge to be shown how Dolph looked to others. Their parents had sent them out of Germany to make them safe; he owed it to them to look after himself; no doubt such qualities as he was blessed with were needed to win the war, but they would be needed even more afterwards, and if their parents survived he ought to be there to help them. "I have spoken about him to Eleanor Rathbone, who is a member of Parliament taking a special interest in the refugees," she wrote, "and also to the MP for East Lothian. But I will not be a party to getting him released from internment so that he can go and throw his life away on some suicide mission."

Inge mistook this for a figure of speech; you had to let him be Dolph, she thought, or what was the point of his being who he was?

Rudi wrote, "I know that it must be hard for David to spend some of the best, perhaps years, of his life behind barbed wire, but he could, if he wanted to, use the time to his advantage." The talents massed on the Isle of Man ranged from Olympic athletes to internationally renowned professors. "He could get as good an education there as at Oxford or Cambridge."

Dolph wrote to her, resorting because of the censor to the private code they had used as children, that he had for the time being given up the idea of trying to save Jews—his latest ambition in the sphere had been guiding people across the Pyrenees—because to get the English to release him he would have to come up with something *they* would want him to do, "and it isn't saving people who make problems for them by wanting to go to Palestine." All he could think of at the moment was becoming a wireless operator, which were two a penny, but he was also learning Flemish, "very useful because it is spoken by few—" a baffling argument.

As far as he and his sister were concerned, the only good thing about his internment was that it allowed them to renew contact with their parents; Inge's letters to and from them passed through the Isle of Man. They were now living in a Jewish neighbourhood, renting two rooms in a houseful of Jews; Inge thought of it as living among friends and believed that they had made the move from choice. Naturally, their mother wrote, they no longer needed most of their belongings and were gradually selling them off; they were now sleeping in their children's beds, having sold their own. Inge, not understanding that this was because her parents' beds would have taken up more space as well as fetched a better price, had it thus spuriously brought home to her that, as with Dolph, the loss was not one-sided. She could not bear to think of her parents as hankering after her, it reduced their intrinsic value; she thought of them as hankering after Dolph and being tactful about it to her and did not blame them: was she not hankering after Dolph too?

It was to him and not to them both that they sent a food parcel; Dolph wrote that he wondered whether they really believed that he was going short or whether they meant to proclaim that they themselves still had more than enough. He shared the wrappers with her but ate all the contents, because it was for him that they had spent their bread-coupons; it had not occurred to Inge before that he might feel as homesick as herself.

When he had been in despair over sending Joachim Meyer to *his* death, Hansi had written ". . . and all I can do for him is knit a jumper to keep him warm against the Atlantic gales. I wish it were my arms I could wrap around him . . ." Inge had been scandalized, because Hansi herself had written that she was not his girlfriend; the time was past when Inge would have welcomed her help to keep him thoroughly loved. He now had an Italian girl, with big breasts which was how he liked them, and, again, black eyes, and absolutely no English: but they were managing to communicate very nicely without words, he wrote. Inge got rid of some of her unfocused hostility, the bilge in her soul, on that Italian girl. Mortified not to have thought, herself, of sending him things—it would have reduced his value in her eyes, if she had believed that *she* could have supplied any of his needs—her pride now made her decide to knit, instead, for Rudi, whose needs she believed she understood and felt urged to gratify.

Even while Dolph had been in Whittingehame she had abstained from telling him all the truth; now she was telling him lies in order to, as Rudi put it, sustain him. It never occurred to her that her brother, this alter ego, would know that when she

74

wrote that Miss Pym understood about his internment and was sympathetic it meant that Inge was reassuring herself that she had not been hurt by whatever Miss Pym had said about it; she was making it worse for them both by preventing him from drawing the sting out of Miss Pym's words for her. But she succeeded in altogether concealing from him the problem of Jesus.

It has to be said in extenuation that Miss Pym gave her a home for ten months before coming out with, "Considering that, the world over, for two thousand years, we Gentiles have found fault with you Jews, don't you think that you Jews must have provided the reason? In nothing else has the whole of humanity, generation after generation, been so much in agreement as in this . . . . Change sides, little girl, come to Jesus!" Before she had started talking they had been listening to the nine o'clock news, always an ordeal for Inge: it made her grow upset for quite other reasons than Miss Pym supposed, and she could not or would not explain herself; but she also got told off when she tried not to listen. Now she rummaged in the attic of her mind, through the Zionist stuff she had been accumulating since Hitler had come to power when she was seven-and-a-half years old; the whole of it was swirling in a flash-flood of emotion.

"Come!" Miss Pym said, kindly, putting a hand out: her right hand which Inge envied because it had never written anything except English. "Come, Jill, let us kneel to Jesus."

She had always envied the Christians their gentle Jesus, a much more approachable God than the Jewish Yahweh, rejected by the Roman world because he demanded not only to be believed in but to be lived up to, and did not promise you an after-life. Especially since, knowing Georgie, she could understand people worshipping the Christ child; she imagined him having been like Georgie: fair-haired, blue-eyed, white-skinned: the Nazi image of the ideal man. She thought of him as the first anti-Semite because of the suffering caused in his name but felt that she did not need Miss Pym to act as go-between: from before she could think she had been on familiar terms with his father.

She had been in a church, once, before she could remember: Dolph, short-haired, round-faced, and rubicund had consulted

75

their grandfather about it and afterwards tried to stop their parents from dismissing the Catholic nursemaid who had taken them. Oh, long before the Nazis dispossessed her of the ground under her feet, the air inside her lungs, humanity's riches had been taboo to her: the baubles on the Christmas tree, the baby in the manger, the perennially tortured man whose blood made you innocent. She would have liked Miss Pym's church better if it had been ornamented with gipsy-like abandon: or she believed that the chill she felt as she entered, as if it were snowing inside her, was caused by its visual austerity rather than by the absence of the God she knew. Nothing that had ever happened to her in Nazi Germany had made her feel as cast out as the prim little smile of her mentor, her stand-in-mother, which told her that before she could be at home in this Eden she would have to stop being who she was and give up all she had. In her ignorance, she did not even know that the alien-sounding psalms about her ears were merely English translations of the Hebrew poems which belonged to her because they had been written by her ancestors.

Miss Pym, seeing her so moved, whispered, "Jesus wants you."

Not long before the summer holidays, when Inge had been living with her for almost a year, Miss Pym bought her a handbag; allowed, within limits, to choose, Inge got a grey shoulder-bag. It was so cheap that it did not even include a purse, but she was pleased with it: she had once had a toy one rather like it, and none since. It was a present for her fifteenth birthday, bought in anticipation because she needed it for travelling.

As in the previous year, with Mother, looking over Inge's clothes led to an argument about what to do with all the things she had brought from home and grown out of. "We could send them to the Children's Shelter," Miss Pym suggested and Inge, imagining it as a subterranean Dovercourt, instantly agreed. She cut that umbilical cord blindfold, without even taking another look at what was inside the suitcase before handing it over.

The rest of her belongings, amounting to not all that much, were to be packed in her English suitcase; when Inge questioned taking her winter clothes for an August stay in the Cotswold Hills—they were to spend a fortnight in a guest-house kept by

76

nuns—Miss Pym told her, "You'll be remaining in the convent."

Inge misunderstood: believed that Miss Pym meant for the rest of her life, and all the hankering she had felt for Jesus, a homesickness almost, cleared away like fog: how could she ever have thought of doing this to her mother, who when she had first got married had kept kosher house, whose father had laid *tefillin* every morning and had had a barber in to shave him on the Sabbath; how could she have thought of doing this to Dolph, who called himself an agnostic but had been circumcised and barmitzvah-ed—"topped and tailed", their father had called it, making a joke of it. Calling the Nazis his stick and his children carrots, their father had made a joke of relearning to be a Jew. And supposing Rudi's relations vetoed his marrying a Jewess who had converted? But no: if Miss Pym had her way she would never get married, never have babies; as Christ's bride she would no doubt not even be allowed to write her Jewish poems.

Rudi was to laugh at her: how could she have been so naive as to believe that Miss Pym had such absolute powers, as if she had been the witch in the gingerbread house in the forest? She had read too deeply in *Jane Eyre*, who had been unable to escape being sent to Lowood or to get away from it for years and years . . . . Inge's first thought, as throughout her life in moments of crises, was that she would kill herself; her second thought was that she would run away.

She decided not to try and run to Dolph, partly because of the authorities but mainly because he wasn't Atlas. She could not run to Mother and Dad who, to be rid of her, had handed her over to Miss Pym and were also Christians and for all she knew might approve of her being translated into a nun. She thought, briefly, of making for Whittingehame and Hansi, and, more briefly still, of making for Jean Crowther in London: after nineteen months in England there was nobody else she knew—except Rudi. Rudi was building army camps in Yorkshire; he was stationed in Sedbergh which she believed was near Leeds because he had written to her of visiting there and seeing a Yiddish play.

She rode the rapids of the situation on a raft of words. Before she was aware that her mind was made up, before she took pen and paper, she was composing, "Since you find it so disagreeable that I am a Jew, which I am and must be, I am going away. Please believe me that I am grateful to you for—" here she hesitated, briefly, before rejecting, "giving me a home", which was untrue, in favour of, "looking after me", which felt untrue and sounded too personal, but she was not going to call a flat with a crucifix in it, home. She added, "Please believe me that I am now old enough to look after myself—" by which she meant to say that she wanted to have nothing more to do with Miss Pym. Miss Pym did not hold with using the same words twice in one paragraph, but Inge thought the double "please believe me" nicely conveyed without being offensive the root of their incompatibility.

She got away while Miss Pym was having her hair done. She was now almost the age Dolph had been when they left home; her suitcase was almost the size and weight his had been then, but she was not as strong, and it, instead of being companionable, was a burden; only the thought of what Rudi would say stopped her from leaving it behind.

Did she have to go into London, she enquired at the ticket office, before she could get a train to Leeds? Which of the main stations would she have to go to? She felt so grown up, felt poised on the springboard of life: was for once aware of how she must look to others: a slip of a girl with long dark hair, a face too delicately featured and pale for its robust roundness and with large slate-grey eyes; it was their heavy-lidded sadness which branded her as a Jew. She looked more self-important than she knew and was frowning: worried that Miss Pym would find the note too soon and come after her and as always when she got into a state her accent grew more pronounced. "Would you please repeat that, Miss," the man in the ticket office said, looking not at her but over her shoulder, and who was behind her was not another traveller but a policeman.

He said, "Would you mind coming over here, Miss," but it was not a question, because she did mind and he took her, by the elbow, out of the queue to stand under a poster saying, *Be like Dad, keep Mum*, which after five terms in an English school she still did not understand. The policeman was asking her why she was going to Leeds or rather—she realized—why she was wanting to go there.

Because Rudi had been in trouble with the police she thought it better, for his sake, not to mention him. She invented an aunt, and a name for her, and an address—and too late remembered that she had not changed the label on her suitcase. Looking at it, the policeman asked her, "Is this not your case then, Miss?" He asked for her identity card. While she was getting it out of her new grey shoulder-bag, he asked her how old she was. "Fifteen," she answered, though she would not be that until the end of August—and too late remembered that being a refugee was like being in Looking-Glass Country: for her it would probably be better to be younger. "Fourteen," she corrected herself, in a small voice; even the two syllables sounded as if she had only just arrived. The policeman asked for her Alien's Registration Book.

"That's two lies you've told me," he pointed out, kindly: she would not have been afraid of him if it had not been for what had happened to Rudi. It would not have mattered, if she could not have imagined worse things being done to her than being sent to the Isle of Man—to which, indeed, she would have said, hurray!—or even being put on another *Arandora Star*, which would have had the advantage of putting an end to her. The policeman was saying that he intended taking her home.

"My home is in Germany!" she exclaimed, loudly enough for people to feel justified in showing that she was attracting their attention. "To this address it gives here," the policeman said, with more understanding than she felt she had the right to expect. It emboldened her to say, "No, please don't. Please let me go to my previous address." She was not aware, as the Englishman may have been, of what pathos there was in someone being so emotional about so impersonal a destination.

As they reached the house, Inge hung back and the policeman wanted to take another look at her papers but she was sure: the eleven months she had spent with Miss Pym seemed to her like eleven years, but she felt as if the Sparrows, with whom she had spent eight months, had almost brought her up; her reluctance was due to her fear that, after all this time, Dad would not recognize her.

It was she who, almost, did not recognize him: partly because her feelings had shifted her memory of him in the direction of her father, but chiefly because he looked a lot older, and not only because he had come to the door without his teeth in. It made the joy on his face look akin to horror; as if she were the last person he would have wanted to see, Inge thought. "My girl!" he exclaimed, offering her his arms; she threw herself forward to fill them, more than she knew.

"What is it, Johnnie?" Mother's voice called from upstairs.

Inge burst into tears.

She cried because it was a familiar voice, cried when she realized that she had responded to it with the love which belonged to another, and because she had not expected it of Mother that she would come home again and not want her back, and because she was about to see Georgie, and because he would not remember her and she would have to start all over again making him love her, and because now she did not have to face the unknown Leeds but could stay here, which was next best to returning home.

"Mother!" Dad bawled over his shoulder. "Look who's here!"

Inge had not remembered that she looked quite so old.

She came, as if her ankles were failing her, hand over hand holding on to the banister, not quite to the bottom of the stairs and stood there woebegone. Inge went to her and they cried into each other. "What a sad meeting," Mother said; she ought to have called it a reunion, Inge thought, and confusedly made allowances for her because they had started off not speaking the same language. She believed that they, too, had forgotten what it had been like, and now that they were reminded they were sorry for having rejected her—and so they ought to be but she was not gloating. Her heart-buds opening, she was impatient for Georgie; if she did not ask for him it was because she did not want Mother and Dad to be hurt by seeing that he was more important to her than they were.

"Let's go into the kitchen, love, and make Mother a nice cup of tea," Dad said, having dealt with the policeman. As they came together in the doorway, he hugged her once more, saying, "My Inge!"

80

"Inge," she echoed, moved. "Nobody calls me that now."—"Then Jill if you prefer," Dad said, and she was his, *mit Haut und Haaren*, for having remembered the name, quite forgetting that it was he who had given it to her. "Let me!" she exclaimed and dashed to the sink to fill the kettle, taking possession again. Then she said, happily, "I'll just go up and see Georgie." She assumed that he was asleep in his bed or she would have heard him.

"No!" the parents exclaimed together.

"No?" she echoed, and looked from the one to the other, the one to the other, reading their faces as if she were their true daughter. "Isn't he here, then?" she asked, to make it easier for them.

"Sit down, love," Dad said, himself sitting down at the table. She sat down and looked round the kitchen, suddenly unfamiliar because it was uncluttered: no high-chair, no bottles, no nappies drying, no toys: he must have remained with his uncle. Inge swallowed and thought, that's what people call swallowing your disappointment, and bravely tried to be glad on his behalf, because of course he would be much better off living out in the country and away from the bombs. "You see we lost him," Dad said.

She could not take it in: imagined him crawling—no, it would be toddling by now, across alien meadows, tumbling over molehills, little enough to be scared even of sheep and to be lured like Red Riding Hood by picking flowers further and further until, his face grubby with tears and snot, he would, little half-tame creature, crawl into hiding instead of staying where he could be found . . . . She had the impulse to run and look for him.

"Meningitis," Mother said.

Now Inge understood why, before, she had called Dad, Johnnie. She stayed where she was but offered her hands across the table, one to the left for Dad and one to the right for Mother. That was why they had not got in touch with her when Mother got back, they explained: to spare her knowing it. "But it was wrong of us," Dad said. "Maybe that's why you were given to us in the first place."

Some nursemaid had once cut an orange for Inge *across* the

segments and then exclaimed, "What a peculiar orange!" She was reminded of it by the view of the world Dad's words showed her: as if Hitler had happened so that she could fill Georgie's place. "Oh no!" she exclaimed without taking thought. "I'm on my way to Leeds, you see . . ." and she elaborated the lies that had started at the station, until they had taken her safely beyond the reefs of childhood.

FOUR

AUGUST–OCTOBER 1940

(The Duchamps)

"GOOD FOR YOU!" her brother wrote from the Isle of Man. "It is much better to make one's own mistakes." He had crossed out "mistakes" and written above it "decisions", and in the margin apologized for trying to be clever, like Rudi; she believed that this meant that he thought himself—and he ought to know—not as intelligent as Rudi, who had found it easier to get released from internment to help the war effort. She often misread his letters, doubting his English because he spoke it so badly and had not had her advantage of going to school in England. He wrote that when they were children he had sometimes wished that she were a boy—she had suspected as much—and so it served him right if now he sometimes found himself wishing that he were a girl, to be of more use to her. "You must not lose touch with Hansi," he wrote, issuing a commandment; he thanked her for copying out what Hansi had written and commented, "It's more than her arms she wants to wrap around me." Inge had no idea what he meant.

She had not realized, when she had walked out on Miss Pym, that, with her Alien's Registration Book and her no longer valid German passport branded with a large red J, she was not allowed to travel about wartime England as she pleased; she needed to get permission from the police in Leeds before she could go there. It made time for an answer from Rudi: he could not promise to meet her at the station because, alas, just now he was not his own master. Would she believe him if he said that he would rather kiss her hand than shovel cement? He enclosed ten shillings and apologized for not sending more; she did not know then that since his contretemps with the police his relations had been withholding his allowance. He had gone to some trouble, he wrote—rightly believing that she needed to be made to feel valued even more than she needed to be loved—to find out just where she stood: that clause in her Alien's Registration Book about not taking employment paid or unpaid no longer applied: she would be allowed to take any job for which there was no native labourer (the term made her smile as it was meant to do); this aspect of her plight had not even occurred to her. He went on to remind her that girls of her age were usually still living at home: she must not expect to be able to earn a living wage. He knew that this was not the future she had envisaged for herself when leaving home, but going into service—until she was old enough to join the services—would provide her with a roof over her head and three square (he hoped) meals a day, and give her time to look about for something better. He enclosed the address of a household where, he happened to know, she was needed; he knew nothing of the woman except that she wore WVS uniform while pouring sustaining cups of English opium to cheerless soldiery—Inge would recognize the Brobdingnagian brown enamel teapot from Dovercourt. He also sent her the address of the refugee committee, and told her to look out for the insurance office a few doors along: it had a brass plate saying *Refuge Assurance* and he knew of someone who had gone in there under the impression that this was where refugees were reassured. In a postscript he added that he did not know when he would see her: he had just been informed that he was to be posted to Scotland; they would have to send each other their new addresses through David.

Looking for the brass plate gave her something to do before facing the ordeal of explaining herself to strangers; to know what to expect of even a few square inches of Leeds was a help and to find it was, yes, reassuring; the sight of it made her feel that at least she could manage better than some—which was as Rudi had intended.

She was still wavering across the cracks in the pavement which must have served as omens to generations of schoolchildren—the street was an old residential one—when she saw two men coming out of a door like all the others; but they were refugees, she was sure of it without knowing why. There was nothing to tell her that theirs was the house she wanted: the fact that the office was so surreptitious made her think that everyone must be as ashamed as she was of being a refugee; but the two men broke out in loud voices, speaking German, with the gestures of Jews, and Inge, thinking, from where do they take the courage? not wanting to belong with them, either, ran away from there too.

She had travelled overnight, so as to arrive in the early hours of the morning and have a whole day in which to find her next bed; it was not yet noon when she reached the other address which Rudi had given her, in a suburb. The witch's gingerbread house Inge thought when she saw it; her father's taste was austere but he might have drawn something like this, with gables and leaded mullioned windows, to please his romantic daughter. The gardens—lawns with flower-beds, flowering bushes and some trees—were under a spell of neglect which had only just been cast.

You did not go up to the front door of such a house, Inge thought, if you were a refugee. She was turning away, discouraged but not to the dregs, and she might have rallied to look for the servants' entrance. A car drew up behind her and a woman in a green suit, with badges, and a schoolgirl's hat, also green, wound the window down further to call out to her, "I hope I didn't keep you waiting, I'm so glad you've come! Just open the gates for me, will you?" Not knowing that Mrs Duchamp believed that she had been sent by the agency which tried to keep her supplied, Inge, opening the wrought iron gates to the drive, thought the reception she got a sort of miracle.

By the time Mrs Duchamp—who looked born to the house—had parked her car, she knew that Inge's name was Jill, knew her age—"It can't be helped," she said to that—and that her suitcase was still at the station. She herself had just come from there, Mrs Duchamp told her, she had taken the early shift; not knowing that she was doing her war work for petrol and prestige, Inge thought, oh, how kind-hearted she must be!

The entrance hall had a glass wall and was full of pot plants. "These are my babies," Mrs Duchamp said, and enchanted Inge by adding, "I have green thumbs." The floor was of red tiles. "They only need scrubbing in dirty weather," Mrs Duchamp said. "Now you can get away with polishing them once a week." It sounded to Inge like connivance to make light work. Going on, Mrs Duchamp said, "The house doesn't get dirty with just the two of us." Inge thought she meant, the two of them.

Of course, Inge thought, if I can go in it can't be all that marvellous—because the inside of the house was disappointing: altogether too fussy and not to the taste with which her parents had saddled her for life; she did not realize that everything was antique and valuable. "Your first task in the morning is to come in here and straighten it for breakfast," Mrs Duchamp said, showing her the room now used for all purposes because there was a war on. With a gesture at the fireplace she added, "In the winter of course your first task is to start the fire." That was the second time she had mentioned the winter and Inge was reassured: this was her fourth address in less than two years.

The kitchen was modern, and spotless; Inge believed that it would delight her to keep it like that. "This is your radio," Mrs Duchamp said, turning it on for her, briefly, to Dovercourt-like dance-music. "You won't have to do any cooking, I do it all." It moved Inge to tears, what Mrs Duchamp was willing to do for her.

The stairs were the poorest feature of the house: too narrow and too steep; her father would have designed better. Like a mole on a cheek, Inge thought: that the house was flawed made her the more willing to take care of it—houses were more reliable than people. She stroked the wall and Mrs Duchamp exclaimed, "Don't do that!" in a tone so different that Inge looked about for what perhaps the cat was doing. "We won't be able to redecorate until this wretched war is over." It was not said as if she meant that then she and Inge would do it together. "Take your hand off the wall, child!" Inge forgave her for shouting at her because she had called her, child.

In the master bedroom she realized that there was a Mr Duchamp, but had no time to think about him because Mrs Duchamp was saying, "Your first task in the morning is to bring the tea-tray." Even being a domestic servant was going to be more difficult than she had supposed. Better make a clean breast of it, she thought, and said, "I haven't any experience."

They stood at the top of the poor stairs and discussed her life until Mrs Duchamp, to put an end to the flood, told her, "I'm sure we shall get on like a house on fire," and Inge was willing to love her for pandering to her passion for idioms so early on in their relationship. "That's my son's room," Mrs Duchamp said, passing a door. "My little baby plays with those terrible bombers. You will have seen his photograph downstairs." Inge did not like to say that she had not noticed it. "I hope he won't object to my employing the sister of a political suspect," Mrs Duchamp said and Inge, who thought that she had not explained herself properly, drew breath for another try. Mrs Duchamp said, "Perhaps we'd better keep that our little secret."—"I won't tell him," Inge promised, adding, "unless he asks me." She wasn't going to be a Peter. Mrs Duchamp gave a laugh. "Why should he ask you? He won't even notice you, you funny girl!" Inge wished that she had not called her that without knowing why she objected to it so strongly.

"And this is your room," Mrs Duchamp said, showing it to her. Inge did not know what to look at first: the bed had a padded headboard and was covered with a pale blue, embroidered, satin bedspread; there was a glass-topped dressing-table —she had never owned the use of a dressing-table in her life; the curtains were of pale blue linen patterned with lilies-of-the-valley and the view was of the garden and the trees beyond. Mrs Duchamp must be the nicest woman on earth, Inge thought, to have prepared such a room for a stranger.

"You can use this as your bathroom," Mrs Duchamp said, showing it to her; there were traces of male occupation. "Of course you won't use it when my son is on leave."—"No of course not," Inge agreed hastily, without wondering what she would do then.

Mrs Duchamp looked at her little gold watch and after exclaiming at the hour said, "It's high time we had lunch!" She was fond of using the royal we but Inge did not yet know it and felt hot gratitude, not because she was hungry, though she was, but because she believed that she was being shown consideration.

They returned not to the kitchen but to the hall. "Well," Mrs Duchamp asked, "do you want the job?" Inge believed that she had already got it. "You have no experience," Mrs Duchamp reminded her. "And you ought to have references." Inge did not know what she meant but did not say so. "How do I know that you are who you say you are?" Inge was side-tracked into thinking of Dolph, who had once explained to her the futility of answering such a question. "Well?" Mrs Duchamp continued in monologue. "What shall I pay you, child?" Inge was wondering whether to tell her that she was willing to be her house-daughter—the term used by Jews in Germany for girls in her position—in exchange for pocket-money—which was what she would have got in Germany. "Well, you funny girl," Mrs Duchamp persisted, "how much are you worth?" It was on the tip of Inge's tongue to say, as much as yourself; the words she kept back came out of her eyes as tears. "Of course it's all found," Mrs Duchamp was saying; Inge did not know what this meant. "Say half a guinea a week," Mrs Duchamp offered. Trying to remember how much this was—having had to learn so much she had not learned everything—Inge did not bargain, and did not hear her say that she could have one afternoon and one evening off, in a week.

She was told to take her coat off; she went to hang it on the hallstand with the others. Mrs Duchamp told her, irritably, "Not there! It belongs on the hook by the back door," and Inge took it there, not so much upset at being relegated as she was happy that she belonged.

Mrs Duchamp said that she would show her how to lay the table and Inge thought, does she think I was raised in a stable? but she found that she needed to be shown; they laid one place only and she thought, of course, she has no food in the house for me, she wasn't expecting me—before she understood that she was to eat in the kitchen. "Let me have your ration-book," Mrs Duchamp said. "I've found that servants are not to be trusted with money. But you'll come with me to the shops, this afternoon, to carry the bags." She showed Inge her place in the larder: she would have her own butter and sugar dishes, her own pot of jam. "We'll buy something you don't like," Mrs Duchamp told her, "you'll find that it goes further," and added, "For now you may borrow some of the Doctor's." If Inge had not been so taken with the house, she would have noticed his brass plate beside the gate. (It was some time before she found out where his surgery was: in Jewish Chapeltown.)

She was told to cut the bread—something which had always been done for her, even by—especially by—Miss Pym. She was so anxious to do it well and quickly that the loaf flew out of her hand and skidded across the floor. She stood there, flushed and aghast, until Mrs Duchamp told her, equably, to pick it up, adding, "You'd better get the vacuum cleaner out or we'll be treading the crumbs into the carpets." Inge picked the loaf up and again just stood there. "Get a move on!" Mrs Duchamp exclaimed and Inge reminded her that she did not know where it was. "Well, you funny girl, find it!" When she had done so, and was struggling to put it together, Mrs Duchamp asked her, "Doesn't your mother have a vacuum cleaner? Your people have such a reputation for cleanliness!" It astonished Inge, who had seen slogans about dirty Jews written up, in two languages; she was to find that, in spite of all her explanations, Mrs Duchamp persisted in considering her a German.

When the Doctor heard Jill going on about it, he stationed himself behind his wife and shook his head at her, sadly, to convey that it was of no use; he was too soft-hearted to tell her that his wife hated Jews, had to believe as she did, so as to employ her, because servants were becoming hard to get. When Jill was introduced to him, he took one swift, omniscient look at her and grunted, "You're anaemic," but it was only the exhaustion of her overnight journey and the harrowing of her by Leeds. Nevertheless, he gave her a sweet-tasting tonic, and included her among the recipients of the oranges and bars of chocolate given to him by devoted patients. He teased her, gently, whenever he saw her, a brainy child, going so solemn-eyed about her trivial adult chores. The impulse to smash things which had been with her since Dovercourt now manifested itself in clumsiness; whenever she broke dishes—those symbols of familial domesticity—Mrs Duchamp deducted sixpence from her wages, and stood over her while she cleaned up with dustpan and brush because sherds would have damaged the vacuum cleaner; the Doctor, if he happened to be at home, winked at her behind his wife's back and challenged her to cut herself to prove to them all that her blood was as blue as their own. She was grateful to him for the joke but did not understand it; both Dolph and Rudi wrote telling her what it meant.

The poor stairs had to be done with dustpan and brush because the vacuum cleaner might have damaged the banister; she had just started on them, one mid-morning, when someone came to the front door. It was one of her duties to answer it. She did not recognize the son of the house because he had grown a moustache and was not as tall as she had expected—both his parents were tall; she had the impression that he would have walked through her if she had not got out of his way. The photograph of him on the living-room mantelshelf was a black and white one and she had also been unprepared for his Aryan colouring; his mother's hair was blond but it was dyed. The welcome he got from her reminded Inge of Dolph returning from his scout camp and caused her a passionate pang of homesickness for her brother. Struggling against her tears, she left off her eavesdropping to get on with sweeping the stairs.

When she heard him crossing the hall, she was low enough for him not to be able to look up her skirt; she thought, he can bloody well wait until I have done; but he didn't: trying to get past her, he put a hand on her rump. With the carpet brush firmly in her hand, she turned sharply; it gave him a glancing blow across the right temple. His Nazi-blue eyes met her eyes in astonishment.

His mother had followed him into the hall and seen what happened; she began to scream at Jill, "You bloody little Hun! We were right to suspect you!" To her son she said, "We've thought all along that she was up to no good, with her sob-story about being Jewish. Let us see, my poor baby, what that wicked girl has done to you, before we phone the police." The squadron-leader looked from the one to the other and to Inge's mortification said, "She looks Jewish to me." He had inherited his father's slow baritone.

Mrs Duchamp turned back to Inge and screamed, "Why did you do it?"

Inge thought that, considering how accident-prone she had become, it was a silly question. She wanted the handsome airman to understand that it was at least partly his own fault, but as always when she was in a state her English deserted her: left her without a polite word for her rump, and the "on" she meant to use came out as "up", so that what she said was, "He put his hand up my skirt." Even before she had completed the phrase she was horrified by it: only idiots, Dolph had taught her, told lies that they couldn't get away with. She glanced at the young man and, thinking that he deserved better, bolted up to her room and locked the door.

"These foreigners are all the same!" she could hear Mrs Duchamp screaming. "We took her in off the street and gave her a home and this is how she repays us!" Sebastian's answers were too low for her to make out. Listening to the antiphony of alarm and balsam, Inge burst into tears.

There was some coming and going on the stairs and in the passage, then silence, then a gentle knock on her door. "Please open up, I need to speak with you."

"Go away!" Inge bawled, wishing at once that she hadn't: silence would have been better. After a moment he knocked again. "Jill? I've got to speak with you, it's important." What could he want with her? His mother obviously thought her not even good enough to be raped by him. She wondered if he had gone, when he asked, "What are you doing in there?" What did he think she was doing? It gave her the idea of smashing her room up; with the intention of breaking the mirror she picked up her hairbrush and could not make herself throw it. Seeing the housemaid's black and white uniform topped by her own wild and bewildered face reminded her of those joke photographs in which people show their heads above cardboard bodies; it started her laughing, hysterically.

That sent him away: down the stairs; but after a while he came back and knocked again. "Open up, I've brought you a cup of tea." That started her laughing again, less crazily this time, and he said, "Don't think that I made it because I wanted one. I'm drinking whisky!" To prove it he rapped the bottle against the door. He called out, "I'm sitting across your threshold like one of King Arthur's knights. You can't stay in there for ever. I need your help." It sounded so improbable that she was terrified.

"Jill?" he asked. "Is that what your brother calls you?" That made her open up.

His mother had told him about her brother, warning him to be careful of what he said in front of her. "I need you to do me a favour," he said. "Don't give notice—and I won't blame you if you do—but don't give notice until after I've gone, I only have forty-eight hours." He needed to ask his mother for money to settle a debt, and if Jill gave notice she would be in such a paddy that she wouldn't give it to him, and she would tell his father not to give it to him either, and his father always did as his mother said for the sake of peace.

"I hadn't thought of giving notice," Inge told him, truthfully: she could not have faced another uprooting so soon. "I like this house." He gave her a baffled look, offered her his bottle and when she shook her head, struck dumb by the sudden recollection of what had happened on the stairs, he raised it to her, as Dolph had once raised a milk bottle, before putting it to his lips; he had inherited his father's generous mouth.

Later that day, when she remembered, she went to clear her things out of his bathroom: they had already been taken and put on her dressing-table. It did not really matter: there was a basin in the downstairs lavatory, she could manage for forty-eight hours. But, behind her back, her things migrated back on to Sebastian's shelves; she overheard him saying to his mother, "It's her home as much as mine, at least for the moment." It made it necessary for her to shut herself away again, to hide her tears. After that, both she and Mrs Duchamp behaved as if nothing had happened.

She was anxious to apologize to him or at least to explain how that accusation had come about but he did not give her the chance; he disappeared again without even telling her if he had got his money and she tried not to think about him: not knowing how many sorties he had flown she could not work out his life-expectancy but it could not have been long.

He came again at the beginning of September, looking devastated. He went upstairs to his room and locked himself in and would not come out again, or answer his mother, or eat; she phoned the butcher and sent Inge in a taxi to fetch the meat and spent all afternoon in the kitchen. If Sebastian was in a state, so was his mother by the time the Doctor came home.

The Doctor thought, he told Jill, that he must have lost one, or more than one, of his friends; at one point he sat down on a chair in the passage and talked at him through the door. Inge was tired enough—it had been her afternoon for doing the ironing—to have fallen asleep when he roused her to make Mrs Duchamp a cup of lemon tea; he seemed the same as always but normally he would have got it for her himself. Inge went downstairs wondering at the usage of words: the English (the Germans, too, but she had been too young to hear them) talked about losing people as if they wished to hold themselves responsible for their death; she was wondering what Freud had made of that, what Rudi would say, when she thought that she heard a noise in the living-room. Afterwards, she could not remember being scared: she was probably half-asleep; but she remembered being amused at the thought, as she crossed the hall, that Dolph would have to learn to say that he had *lost* her—and remembering too late that there were worse things people could do to you than kill you.

She switched the light on and at once switched it off again: partly it was a reflex, after a year of war, because she had seen that the window was not blacked-out; the light had shown her Sebastian standing in front of it with his back to her.

He was to tell that he had known who it was because neither of his parents "would have tried to crawl back into the woodwork."—"Jill . . ." he said, questioningly. "Will you see if you can get my father to come down here, without my mother?" She thought that it was the saddest sentence she had ever heard: sad for Mrs Duchamp. She said, "I'll try," but went on standing there until she had worked up the courage to ask if there were anything she could do for him. With his terrible patience—learned from his father or perhaps it had been taught to them both by Mrs Duchamp—he repeated, as if he believed that she had not heard him the first time, "Will you see if you can get my father to come down here, without my mother?" and she repeated that she would try, and went back to the kitchen.

She was wide awake now: galvanized by the drama. Sebastian was still a stranger to her at this time—was to remain a stranger but that was not how it was to seem to her—if she had special feelings for someone in that household, then, they were for the Doctor; it was him whom she did not want to fail. Mrs Duchamp would stay upstairs, she thought, if he were summoned for Jill's sake.

She could have pretended to faint but then she could not have called him. She could pretend to have hurt herself, but as an excuse for getting the Doctor downstairs she would have to have something to show. She was thinking this as she took up the knife and the lemon and she cut herself on purpose—but, with her refugee clumsiness, more seriously than she had intended. She grabbed a teacloth: it would be she who would have to clean up the blood, and with real tears in her eyes—though some were of vexation and others, half-stale ones, were not for herself— she ran up the stairs; by the time she got to the landing the teacloth was theatrically bloody.

"The girl who shed her blood for me," Sebastian called her, later on in that week when he had pulled himself together and, one evening, when both his parents were out, joined her in the kitchen where she sat reading because the light there was better than in her room; she had believed that she was alone in the house. He had brought his bottle with him. "No, thank you, it makes me weepy," she said when he offered it to her, because that was what had happened when the Doctor had given her a tiny bottle of champagne on hearing that she had never tasted it.

"If I had had a life like yours I'd be weeping all the time," Sebastian said. Inge thought this unfair: it wasn't her fault that she had not had his advantages; she asked, belligerently, "What's wrong with it?" To sit down, he raised a leg as if to mount a bicycle and straddled a chair; she had seen it done in films but never in life. He rested his hands on the back and his chin on the backs of his hands and gazed at her. "You don't think that what happened to you is a catastrophe?" She thought he meant that its effect on her had been catastrophic, and flushed, and after a moment argued, "But nothing's happened to me!" thinking of camps, concentration and internment ones.

"That you lost your home—" he began, and started her giggling; he stared at her, smoothing his shaggy Nazi hair back with both hands which was one of his gestures, and said, softly, "You're right to laugh at me, I don't have to tell you! But, you know, people are always doing it. You'd be surprised at the number of people who have told me what I must have been feeling while I . . ." She looked over her shoulder to see what he was looking at and was no wiser; his face had grown ashen.

After a silence which lasted for so long that she picked up her book, he said, "I pilot a bomber." He made it sound like something he had never told anyone and she assumed that this was because he would have put it differently if she had been English. She opened her book and found her place.

"Jill," he called to her softly, after she had read half a page or so without taking in a word, "Are you not interested in people or are you afraid of them?" She looked up to see if he were perhaps, like his father, trying to tease her, and caught an expression on his face which, she thought, was like Jacob wrestling with the angel. "Don't you want to know, or do you know too much? That business about my putting my hand up your skirt, if you remember, the first time we met . . ." She could feel herself blushing and he looked away from her. "If I asked you very nicely, which is what I'm doing now, would you condescend to explain?" He added, "Perhaps we could help each other."

She had thought of him as adult: his uniform lent him authority and he was quite a few years older than she; but he was only in his early twenties and now, in his old cricket pullover, he looked like a schoolboy who had been left out of the team which he had expected to captain. Thinking that she was more of a resident in the house than he, that he could be said to be visiting her because they were in her kitchen, she may have given him a look he resented because he said, "Jews aren't the only people who have problems, you don't have to be a refugee to feel the odd one out. Do you think that my mother and I speak the same language?"

She thought—for the last time—that he wasn't a patch on her brother: poor little rich boy, he must be in a bad way if he could find no better company than herself. She thought, he's just an older Georgie—and suddenly found that she could talk to him.

She even told him that she meant to become a writer—which was not something she told to everybody. "I'll lend you some books," he said, like his father, instantly helpful, and then smacked his forehead with the heel of his hand—Dolph's gesture—saying, "I must be drunker than I thought, I threw them all out, all that crap about getting married and producing children and growing old . . ." But he had kept his boys' books:

95

she had looked, after she had met him, wondering what he was like inside; she had found a badly made model of a sailing-ship in a place of honour, and now took the opportunity to ask him about it.

"That's the *Bounty*," he told her. "That's how I liked to see myself when I was a boy, as Fletcher Christian." The name was meaningless to her; she might as well still not have known any English, so far was she from understanding him.

He had told his mother to instruct her to keep out of his room while he was on leave—he would not even let her make his bed—but he called her in, the next day or the day after, to show her what books he had. He was again nursing a bottle and she asked him, "Do you always drink so much?"—"Only when I mean to get drunk," he answered, and gave her a look from under his eyebrows such as she was used to from her brother which meant, if you can't take me as I am then let me be, and she thought, as she used to do, who am I to sit in judgement?

But she worried about him. The Doctor daily came into the kitchen to clean his shoes; at the outset Inge had said that her father had never expected his shoes to be cleaned by their maids—in the days when they had had them, and the Doctor had managed to prevent his wife from making an issue of it. Now, without having had the intention, Inge found herself talking to him about people who drank too much and he exclaimed, "Good God, girl, I don't drink as much as all that. Can't even get the stuff nowadays!" It was so skilfully done that it did not occur to her until years later that he must have pretended to misunderstand her; at the time she thought, Sebastian doesn't bother to hide it from me because I'm only his mother's skivvy, but he cares what his father would think . . . . She did not yet even know—perhaps could not, emotionally, afford it—that it wasn't possible to hide things from such a father.

Rudi was to tell her that she had no right to assume that other people, because she did not see them at it, spent less time thinking than she did herself; she believed that it was his drinking which brought about the change she could see in Sebastian in the course of that leave. Towards the end of it he was hardly ever at home. After a day in which she had not seen

96

him at all, she tried in vain to stay awake so as to at least hear
him come in; waking up, later, she checked his toothbrush and
finding it dry went downstairs to make sure that the chain had
been left off the front door. He was not in the house at breakfast
time.

The sudden thought that his leave might already be up made
her blurt out something about it which earned her a swift look
from the Doctor. Mrs Duchamp, glancing through *The Times*,
said, "He'll have stayed out with friends." Inge thought that she
meant, stayed out of bed, and had a vision of the immaculate
squadron-leader in some boom town gutter—most of her spare
time was spent in the cinema; she felt like shaking Mrs
Duchamp out of her complacency.

She was alone in the house when the phone rang, in mid-
morning. She nearly did not answer it. The calls made to the
Doctor did not reach them during surgery hours and it was one
of the ways in which she got her own back on her mistress: it
made Mrs Duchamp's friends think that she was again between
servants. But it occurred to her that it might be for Sebastian. It
was Sebastian.

She told him that his mother was out and he described whom
he wished to speak to, making such an elaborate joke of it that
she almost hung up on him—thinking him drunk—before
realizing that he meant herself. Would she have dinner with
him? She was astonished into asking, why? It was the last
evening of his leave and he needed her help to get through it.
Writing to her some weeks later he was to explain that what had
"got him" about her was her innocence—as in the phrase
"innocent civilians", the corollary of which is that all fighting
men are guilty: Sebastian had the makings of a pacifist. At the
time she thought that he meant that, in her capacity as family
servant, it would be her job, if he should get drunk, to see that
he got home. It was not her night off, she told him. He said that
he would be back in time to take a bath and to square it with his
mother. "I haven't got anything to wear!" she argued but he had
hung up.

"I haven't got anything to wear!" she greeted him before he
was through the front door. He propelled her upstairs, saying,
"I'll choose you something," but she would not let him look, not

97

wanting him to see the fewness of her belongings. Guessing as much, he did not insist, and out of his bitter malaise which she misunderstood began to lecture her: a girl could either dress up in silks and diamonds or pretend that she did not want to: did Jill not have a pair of slacks? "And that hand-made plum-coloured jumper?" They were the only things he had seen her wear, apart from her housemaid's uniform.

While he was having his bath she sat at her dressing-table and made up her face. "Beautiful!" he said when he saw her, but so perfunctorily that only her own low opinion of herself stopped her from being hurt. Instead she felt proud: there wasn't a girl or woman in Leeds who, that evening, would not have been willing to change places with her. He was gazing above her head out of the window at the overcast sky, so wistfully that she was wondering if he were thinking of his death. They were crossing the hall before he pulled himself together enough to take a look at her. He exclaimed, "Good God, why have you got yourself up like a tart?" and dragged her into the kitchen, and, with the washing-up cloth and the wartime hand soap, cleaned her face—as she used to do Georgie's after a messy meal; it was a more caring gesture than Rudi's at Dovercourt.

Walking towards the town, he asked, "Would you rather have a taxi—if we can find one?" She was so confused that she thought that a ride in a taxi—oh luxury!—would make the time pass more quickly and answered, truthfully, that she liked walking. "But you're on your feet all day long!" he exclaimed and she, made invulnerable by so much consideration, light-heartedly reminded him that she was young. "So am I," he said, "or I used to think that I was. I used to think all sorts of things, like thinking moonlight romantic. This fucking war has ruined everything!" He held her back so as to look into her face while he asked her, "Do you mind me using swear-words like that?"—"No," Inge lied, speared by his look as on a roasting-spit; who was she to mind anything about him?

This is what people mean when they talk about life passing like a dream, she thought, finding herself sitting at a table in the most exclusive place she had ever been in, halfway through the best meal she had ever had. Most of her attention had been taken up by the debate raging within her: how could she fall in love with a flyer who would be as dead as Georgie was within a matter of weeks—would experience never teach her anything? A non-Jewish Englishman who in another uniform would have looked like the Nazi ideal of young manhood, with his rough-shod arrogance, his privileged assumptions, his unapproachability? The people around them—most of them airmen, and their girls and wives—were hailing him as Bill. Why did they call him that? Inge asked and he answered, "Because Sebastian isn't a name that makes for conviviality—not a name that makes a man feel a chum."

"I know what conviviality means!" Inge exclaimed indignantly; but it was not long before she made a fool of herself. A crowd came up to talk to "Bill" and mention was made of someone somewhere about to show a blue film. Believing that, like blue blood, it was something aristocratic, and that Sebastian's look at her meant that he did not think her good enough for it—and being a film-addict—she said, brightly, too loudly, "That would be nice!" Everyone started to laugh and since she did not know of her mistake she did not even know that they were laughing at her.

She forgot to feel proud, forgot herself through taking pride in him; the goodwill in that room was as palpable as the cigarette smoke and he was obviously the handsomest, most popular man there—the best-loved, Inge thought, loving him faster so that none should catch up with her. His crew referred to him as their old man, for which she could have hugged each one of them. People were continually stopping by their table to exchange a few words with him; most of them ignored her, which suited her well enough; but it did not occur to her until she talked it over with Rudi that they might have been embarrassed to see their hell-raising "Bill" turn up with someone who looked like a schoolgirl; with her carefree hair and careladen eyes, they did not know what to make of her. Even when she was introduced, he did not explain who she was—she believed that he was ashamed of her being a servant; she still had no idea that he saw her as more than that; though she was right in thinking that he was curbing his drinking because of her presence; he chain-smoked instead.

When a high-ranking officer paused to congratulate him, she

finally realized that he must have done something exceptional, spectacular, before he had come on leave: something he had told his father on the night she had cut her thumb; and had not wanted to tell his mother, and wanted to tell her but did not know how to set about it. Trying to help him, she asked, "What did he mean, when he said that you suffer from a sense of justice?" He looked at her as if he did not know how she had got there, and stood up, saying, "Let's get out of here, I'm sick of the sight of this uniform." She thought that he meant, on others. "The blackout's at least good for something."

It was pitch-dark outside; they stood in the entrance until their eyes adjusted, Sebastian's hand resting lightly on her arm; she felt his touch run through her as if it had got into her blood. "We'll get a taxi," he said, and she said, "No, let's walk," and with the tactlessness which had made Dolph on occasion want to hit her added, "and then you can talk to me." It made her feel close to him in more than the physical sense, that she was able to contradict him and get her own way.

He took her arm as they set out and said, with more tolerance than her brother could have managed, "You talk and I'll listen." But he wouldn't, she thought: he'd go on thinking about whatever it was that made him want to get drunk and it would make him reckless, careless, would make him—she thought as if she believed him to be one who took no thought for his crew— fly into danger and death: and what good was it that her mother had borne her in agony (she used to say) if she could not help him through more than that one measly evening which was practically over? No, she at once corrected herself, if I were Faust I would willingly give my soul just to have met him.

Making bait of her brother, she said, "I think my brother suffers from a sense of justice."

Sebastian's arm jerked as if he had missed a foothold; he asked, "The one on the Isle of Man?" That he did not know that she had no other brother ought to have served her as a warning, but didn't, that they still knew too little about each other. He said, "But he isn't doing anything!"

Inge let go of him, not caring if he were lost to her in the blackout, thinking that Rudi was right when he said that the English were fair only to their own. "What can he do?" she asked indignantly, and said, as if she believed, with the Nazis, in collective responsibility, "You interned him!" Sebastian relieved his feelings with a flow of swear-words some of which she had never yet heard. She thought that he must be cursing her, or her brother, or both of them.

They walked on in silence and he took her arm again to cross a road, and held on to it. He said, "I went to Berlin."

She thought that he meant, before the war; they would have welcomed him there, with his Aryan good looks. Rudi had told her that the English thought of the Germans as their cousins, that the English Establishment rather admired Hitler and had welcomed the Nazis as a bulwark against communism: that explained the appeasement at Munich, and England's unpreparedness for the war; some of Sebastian's remarks which had baffled her would make sense if he were a Nazi sympathiser. For a week she had told herself that he was his father's son; perhaps she was wrong and he was more like his mother.

"I went to Berlin," he repeated, sounding tearful in the dark.

"So you've said."

She heard him sniff and thought, I don't love you, I've never thought of loving you and I'm not going to love you, and found his hand. She and Dolph had once confessed to each other that if they had not been Jewish, they would have liked to have been in the Hitler Youth. Sebastian was saying, "A year ago, when this war started, our chaps who flew the first missions, they dropped leaflets. Of course I've dropped bombs before, but not on civilians, well maybe they killed some civilians but that wasn't what was intended. And as for the argument," he went on while Inge grew breathless as her mind raced to keep up with him, "the argument that the Luftwaffe dropped bombs on London first—what are we fighting this war for, for Christ's sake, if we are no better than they are?" A rhetorical question, Miss Pym would have called that; but perhaps she had been meant to answer it because he asked her, "Do you understand?"

She thought that he meant, understand that he had told her something of national importance, which she must keep secret from that enemy alien her brother. "I won't tell anybody," she said.

Sebastian exclaimed, "You do believe in getting your pound

of flesh, don't you!" She had not done *The Merchant of Venice* in school and did not know what he meant. He freed his hand, to lay it on her shoulder. "I am sorry, that was unforgivable! Will you forgive me?" She did not know what to say and did not want to speak, concentrating on the feel of his thumb stroking her cheek—the most intimate caress she was ever to have from him; for as long as she believed in God she gave him thanks for having let her cherish the moment even while she had it. It passed and he fetched up a sigh and said, "If you had been living in Berlin and hadn't been brought to England—and I certainly can't claim credit for that, that had nothing to do with me—I could have killed you last week. Among the people we killed there must have been children like you. There were certainly women and children, babies, and old men like my grandfather. Even among the Germans there must be people who are innocent."

For the moment, what mattered most to her was that he had lumped her with the children, and did not think her unique but believed that, in Berlin, there was an Inge under every *Haken-kreuz*. As for the rest of what he had told her, she needed time to think about it or rather—and she always tried to be honest at least with herself—she needed to write her thoughts down for Rudi, to see what they were, and get the searchlight of his comments on them.

She had moved to Leeds for his sake, and had not seen him. He had once told Dolph—so Dolph wrote to her, to warn her off, some time before Rudi actually said this to him—that to become independent of his relations he would have to marry an heiress; Inge believed that his leaves were spent looking for one. His letters to her were growing shorter and fewer and beginning to give the impression that he was bored with her: he thought it high time that she should find herself a more suitable boyfriend. He was delighted to hear of Sebastian.

He wrote that David had at last agreed to accept him as a sort of elder brother—leaving what Rudi did with his heart and loins to Rudi though this was not of course said in the letter—would Jill not do the same? It seemed unlikely, because of the war, that the English would chuck her out at the end of the year when her visa expired, but his relations had made enquiries and the Home Office was making no promises, even to enemy aliens serving in the Forces, that they would ever be able to become British subjects or even that they would be allowed to stay on once the war was over. She must find herself a nice Englishman, and produce English children—who would not be able to reach the higher ranks of the civil service or make careers in the navy but at least, in the next war, they would not have to ruin their fingernails in a labour battalion defacing the countryside with concrete but would be given the gun for which her brother, silly boy, was eating his heart out, and be allowed to be cannon-fodder as real soldiers. Besides, would it not be catastrophic for her as a writer, once more to have to start all over again, learning to write in Hebrew? As for Sebastian's lack of life expectancy, he wrote, if she refused to invest her heart without a guarantee of getting dividends then she had better stick to loving diamonds.

He was so nice about being thrown over that she could not do it; she found that she loved even his handwriting: at the sight of its curlicues she wanted to hug him. The Doctor always knew it when she had had one of his letters; he teased her about them. He did not tease her about Sebastian. Cleaning and polishing his shoes past what was needed, he would tell her that Sebastian's latest flame was a tall blonde, or that he now had a red-head called Vera; he was as fickle as—so far as she knew—her brother. She constantly wrote him long passionate letters which she did not send, and occasionally shorter ones—never more than a page and a half, to sustain but not bore him—over which she laboured to make them sound adult and unconcerned; his letters to her were even shorter, rarer, and, she thought, avuncular. She thought, I don't need him to help me love him, I love him as the Jews love Germany without any help from the Germans.

And indeed, she loved him so well that she could not love him better: not even when he wrote that his whole squadron had signed a petition against the arbitrary internment of "enemy aliens".

"He is the dream but you are the reality," she wrote to Rudi and expected that this would please him: he was always telling her to be more realistic; Rudi decided that he owed it to all of them—her and himself and her brother—to disillusion her. Before his next leave, he wrote to her that on his way "home" he would break his journey in Leeds; he had no home: after some indiscretion his relations had forbidden him their houses, and Leeds was not on the way to where he was going; but he could not face the prospect of confronting her with the truth without securing his getaway.

It took her right back to her childhood, to be going to the station in order to meet someone for an hour or two between trains, it embellished her expectations with emotional echoes of which she was unaware: perhaps not even Sebastian could have lived up to them. She was half expecting Rudi to be like Sebastian, since she longed for him just as much, not realizing that he mattered to her chiefly because he stood for continuity, was a link with her brother and through him with home.

He was a vain young man who would break a date—if he did not care about it too much—because of a pimple; but he also prided himself on not doing things by halves. To be in an ill-fitting private's uniform was not enough: he must also arrive unwashed, unshaven, his fine dark eyes bloodshot because, unable to sleep, he had tried to read on the train; he had been chain-smoking and stank of it. Grimly he thought, let Jill have her reality.

But to her, the only thing that mattered was the getting him back: his being there proved that reunions were possible. She ran to him and put her arms about his neck and wetted his abhorrent face with her tears of welcome and kissed him—her stand-in for Dolph—as if she were indeed his little sister—and left him dissatisfied with them both. It took him a few moments to understand that what he was feeling was not that she had offered him too much but that it had not been enough for him.

On a later occasion he was to tell her that when he saw her so fever-eyed, her cheeks looking as if her plum-coloured jumper had let colour on to them, he had a fantasy that she was ill, that he carried her off to the nearest hotel and put her to bed and took care of her like a mother, so that by the time her gender began to matter, they would already have established a physical relationship based on tenderness and trust. But as he, too, experienced life passing like a dream—he and Inge had a lot in common—his good resolution, superceded but undefeated, made him guide her into a snack bar he had discovered on his previous visit to Leeds.

It was not a fit place for her to be in but she did not notice it: all she was concerned with was what was inside her; they slotted themselves one after the other on to the same bench so that they would be able to hear each other without being overheard, and words began to gush out of her like lava from a volcano, unstoppable. When they got their tea, served in thick white mugs and revolting to their continental palates, he said, prompted not by his master-plan but by self-pity, "I must be a comedown after your squadron-leader!"—"Oh no, Rudi!" she protested, eyes shining but not for him. "He isn't like that at all. I never thought that anybody English could be so much like us!" She said us, Rudi's ears told his heart, while she giggled at some delicious memory which was no concern of his. "He even has to change his name like a refugee—why haven't you changed your name, Rudi?" The undrinkable tea, or more likely his jealousy, was giving him heartburn—the word a gem, he thought, for her collection but, desperate to get on to the subject of Rudi, he put it aside to tell her that he had thought of changing it to George, after the king, Robinson, because he just about managed on this island on which he had been cast up, like Crusoe, but no: "I am the only Rudi in the British army, it prevents my being mistaken for anyone else." She hardly gave him time to get it out, so eager was she to continue talking of the dashing Sebastian, fingering and kneading his hand as she spoke as if she believed that it had no feeling; and the perverse Rudi, for the first time in his life and when he least wanted it, found himself sexually volunteering for a female. He looked down at himself in consternation, and spread his knees under the table, as aware of his spurious erection as if he were standing naked; but the girl noticed nothing, having quite forgotten that she had ever loved him.

Searching for a distraction, his eyes encountered those of a sailor, and struck sparks. The boy rose slowly, slenderly, to an astonishing height—making Rudi blush at the thought that the figure itself was phallic; he came over to their table and, producing a bar of chocolate, said, "For your sister." It had been softened by the warmth of his body.

Only then did it occur to Inge that the generous Rudi had arrived empty-handed; to symbolize, he was one day to explain, that he had nothing to give her.

FIVE

NOVEMBER 1940–JULY 1941

(Dolph)

"HANSI IS JOINING the ATS," her brother wrote in September in a letter which took eight weeks to reach her. "She has no self-respect: as an enemy alien she can be nothing more than a dog's-body and bottle-washer. Pfui!" She was doing it for him, he wrote, and he would make her pay for it—he meant that he could foresee causing her grief but did not put it like that so as not to alarm his little sister who would remember his words when the time came but now thought he meant that he would take it out on Hansi; she was beginning to suspect that exile and internment had had a catastrophic effect on him.

When, one early winter afternoon, Hansi presented herself on the Duchamps' doorstep, Inge's first thought was that this must be Sebastian's latest girlfriend; she hoped that he would marry this one: she looked just about good enough for him: there was too much character in her face for it to be pretty, but her colouring was auburn hair and green eyes; she had dimples when she smiled, and a figure like a film star.

"You must be Inge."

Translated out of reality into one of her daydreams, Inge just stood there, smiling back, until her mistress called out, "Who is it, Jill? I thought I heard the doorbell," and came up behind her. The girl soldier extended her hand past Inge to Mrs Duchamp and told that one, "I am her brother's fiancée." The term was in keeping with their setting and Inge believed that that was why Hansi had used it.

It isn't just me, then, Inge thought when Mrs Duchamp, instead of making the expected remark about using the back door, drew Hansi into the house and in the hall clearly considered treating her as her own guest before allowing Jill to claim her and take her off to the kitchen.

"Let me look at you!" Hansi said, holding her at arms' length by the shoulders. "Oh, what a devil David is, he never told me . . ."—"He didn't tell me about you either," Inge said, but she did not mean to imply that Hansi must find her as satisfactory as she found Hansi.

She had come out of her way to see her before visiting David on the Isle of Man, so that she would be able to tell him about her—as if, Inge thought, she would retain any importance when those two godlings met. But anyway, Hansi said, her presence filling the kitchen as much as Sebastian's, she had long been wanting to meet her. "And I you," Inge said, though it would have been truer if she had had an inkling of what to expect: a pre-Raphaelite beauty, Rudi was to call Hansi, and though her appearance helped, that could not have been what made Inge accept her at once as a sort of elder sister: being so famished for relationships also had something to do with it. To her surprise, she found that she did not want to talk about her feelings, lack of practice had made her forget how to do it: she always found it easy enough to put them down on paper. She could not think of anything to say about Sebastian beyond that she loved him, her description of him felt inadequate, was misleading: made Hansi respond with, "Why should you not be good enough for him?" which diminished Sebastian and left Inge more dissatisfied with herself than ever.

It was more fulfilling to talk of her brother, about whom they could believe themselves to be in agreement although they even called him by different names; it reminded Inge of one of those machines they have in fairgrounds for testing your strength: every time one of them said something about him down came the hammer and up went the other's opinion. "He won't talk about his boyhood," Hansi said, stroking Inge's head, commenting, "You have the same obstinate hair." She said, "He won't talk about your parents," and Inge had to think back over what she had said about them, talking of her brother: she did not want to talk about their parents either, not even to him. "They must be rather special people," Hansi said, "to have two such special children." Inge did not think so: had coped with being parted from them for the past two years by persuading herself that they were no great loss to her.

Doubting her doubts, she asked, "You didn't really join up because of my brother, did you?" Hansi laughed, showing her perfect teeth; Inge joined in: laughing not at herself for asking the question but at that conceited ass of a brother who had put it into her head—what wasn't in Dolph that Hansi could see in David? She was saying, "Though I'd give my life for him." Inge regretted her saying it: it was too extravagant, like Hansi's handwriting, and not to be believed; it made her take from then on everything Hansi told her with a pinch of salt. Apart from the obvious reasons for joining up, Hansi explained, which she need hardly spell out, there were advantages: "The English will overlook your being no more than a private—they don't mind stupidity or lack of initiative—but they'll not forgive you for being down at heel. In uniform, and with a foreign accent, they can't place you socially. You saw how that woman dithered."

That was because you look as if you were somebody, Inge thought. She felt, in Hansi's presence, extraordinarily smug about herself and believed that this was to be ascribed to Hansi when really it was because she was at home there and Hansi wasn't; as far as she knew Hansi had no home, except her uniform—and, Inge thought, a grudgingly-let chamber in Dolph's heart.

With the idea of giving Hansi a treat, she knocked on the living-room door and asked if she might show her visitor Sebastian's photograph; Mrs Duchamp told them both to come in and herself handed it to Hansi. Inge was sorry that she could not also show her the family album which she had discovered in a drawer of Mrs Duchamp's escritoire, displaying Sebastian at all the stages of boyhood; she had filched a photograph of him lying, six months old or so and naked, on his tummy on a bearskin: that one not so much because it made him look rather like Georgie as because it was loose and if missed could have fallen out and because she could look at it and think, if he lives to beget a son, that is what he will look like. There was also a photograph of Mrs Duchamp as a gentle-faced flapper, which explained how the perspicacious Doctor could have been misled into believing that she was livable-with, as Inge had been misled when she had first come to the house; she could not regret their mistake because of Sebastian. Thinking, as she did at least once a day, that his mother must have been to him as a baby what Rosie Sparrow had been to Georgie, and trying to recapture, as the woman stood chatting to Hansi, her unprejudiced view of her, she could see her again as agreeable and put that down to Hansi's presence too.

Saying good-bye to Inge, Hansi told her not to fret about her brother: she was going to London: somebody in the government had promised to help her if she were in uniform. Inge opened her mouth to speak, but thought that, under the circumstances, it would be ungracious to charge Hansi with having contradicted herself; urged to come out with it, she grabbed at the first cloud that threatened and asked, instead, "Who is Jean Crowther?"

"Jean Crowther's a shit," Hansi said, sounding not coarse but fastidious; somebody something to do with Intelligence had asked her to provide a character reference for David and she had said that he was hot-tempered. It made Inge smile to hear it: brought him before her as a twelve-year-old in a turkey-paddy; it left her thinking of him as younger than herself.

But after she had been to the Isle of Man Hansi wrote, among other things, that she had been wrong about Jean Crowther: the woman had only done as David would have wished. In his letter, which Hansi carried beyond the wire, he explained that the Free French had wanted to employ him as a courier to their Resistance. "No doubt they need somebody like me and I could have done it," he wrote, "but I am not going to risk my life for *that*!" He did not come into any of the categories which were now being released, but his name was being put forward by friends in high places for something special—though he had little hope of even being considered until next August when he would be eighteen.

He wrote that never never never would he join the British army: he had not Rudi's penchant for savouring his frustrations—Inge had not known that Rudi had or did that. He had friends, Dolph wrote, who had jumped at the chance of joining the Pioneer Corps—as Joachim Meyer had jumped at the chance of going to Canada; to Inge the reference sounded lighthearted, a joke almost, she was astonished at her brother. They—his friends now in uniform—were lumped by the British with ex-convicts and the physically unfit and, all their talents and qualifications ignored, were being used as cheap labour; such soldiers they were that they were not even armed. He was not going to enter a trap in which he could not rise above the rank of sergeant, at the mercy of some toffee-nosed Englishman—she believed that he had invented the expression for her amusement and felt slighted—who would not be able to do half as well whatever it was he would tell someone else to do who could not do it at all—when Dolph could have done it better.

He had chucked learning languages, he wrote—just like that, without any explanation, as if he had been playing school, when she had almost got herself into trouble trying to buy—while the Hitler-Stalin pact was on—the Russian grammar he had asked for; he was continuing to tinker with wireless-sets and getting quite good with them. There was talk of forming a Jewish Brigade and he was willing to join that—but only if it were "better than the mule corps we had last time". Oh Dolph! Inge wailed within her, don't you know, sitting on your arse on the Isle of Man, that there is a war on, that we must all do our bit? She felt certain that if Sebastian were grounded and told, say, to sweep out the hangars, he would just get on with it. She suspected her brother of being not nearly as brave as he liked to pretend—or why didn't he go to France, it would have been a start? She wished that he were where she could fear for his life so that he would not come such a long way behind Sebastian in her thoughts; she was to have her wish granted, with a vengeance.

Thinking better of herself because she was his sister had always felt a bit like pulling herself out of the Jewish quicksands by her own shoelaces; now she was beginning to think, what did I expect: of my brother? She thought that he liked it too well on the Isle of Man. His letters, unlike Rudi's, never dwelt on his physical circumstances, which he thought both unimportant and useful conditioning: when there were not enough beds or blankets to go round, it was he who slept on the floor wrapped in his jacket; when food was short he gave his share to the old and the sick. It looked to Inge as if he were waiting for Jean

Crowther, or Hansi—or Sebastian!—to get him released from internment instead of doing something about it himself.

As an afterthought—did he, too, Inge wondered, lack a sense of proportion, and had Rudi told him so?—he wrote that, no, he would not be marrying Hansi: he was not going to assume responsibilities which would clash with the commitment he had to their parents; Inge thought he meant, the promise he had made to their mother not to let her out of his sight. Oh, the fool, the fool, she cursed him, beating her thighs with her fists, doesn't he realize how lucky he is that Hansi is willing to have him? and felt no gratitude but only scorn that he should think it more important to be a brother than a husband—more than three months past his seventeenth birthday.

Rudi wrote apologizing, again, for making her leave the snack bar without finishing her tea; she was under the impression that he and the sailor had known each other and had no idea of what had passed between them. In retrospect, she could see that she had treated him badly, refusing to recognize that he was miserable when he was making her so happy by being there after such a long time when she had so much to tell him who understood her so well, "no doubt better than Sebastian," she wrote, meaning it, and, trying to play up to him, added, "But who wants to be totally understood?" Rudi didn't; he did not blame her that she no longer loved him; as Inge might have thought, if he had been Jill he would not have loved Rudi either. But he wanted her to feel something for him, and if not love what else was there that she—who had ceased to admire her heroic brother—could feel for him except pity? He was chilled through to the marrow of his bones, he wrote, he had open sores on his fingers: chilblains or infected callouses, who could tell and who cared? and he had corns on both his little toes. He had been promised a stripe but had not got it; a senior officer who had been his friend now had it in for him. "But you don't want to hear about my troubles," he wrote, "you have enough of your own," and went on for another page and a half about the bleakness of his life. He was right to fear that she would lose patience with him: she wished that Sebastian would provide her with no greater worries. Rudi had once tried to explain to her that if someone is unhappy enough to want to kill himself then the cause cannot be said to be insufficient; she thought that he was making mountains out of molehills, and wrote and told him so.

Of course she believed that he was prompted by malice when he began his next letter with the question, "Are you intending to remain a housemaid for ever?" She was living like a prisoner with an occasional hour or two of parole, he pointed out; it was high time that she found herself something more suitable to do, and mixed more with people. She could continue her education at evening classes, where she would find other people like herself—he was trying to disarm the unknown for her but she believed that it was meant as an insult: they had assured each other that they were unique; he was subverting her allies, words, to take his revenge. She might even advance to a wing-commander, he wrote; as for the army, nothing less than a colonel would do. He did not recommend the navy: sailors did not know where to keep their chocolate; he was trying to live down one of the most ghastly moments of his appalling life, but she felt scornful of his attempts to be funny when they did not come off. This beastly world, he wrote, which exposed his nose to the wintry elements until he looked like a drunkard, would not for ever guard David as if he were the crown jewels. "After all he has done to help you make yourself the girl you are, you owe it to him to provide him with a home to come home to." Trust Rudi.

That was not the end of the letter and as he had not yet mentioned Sebastian, she dreaded reading on; but Rudi, like the Doctor, knew where to draw the line. If she meant anything to Sebastian, he wrote, leaving his parents' house would make no difference: on the contrary, it would help him to get to know her better if he could see her against a background of her own.

On her next afternoon off she went to the labour exchange; she had walked round the block twice before she could make herself go in: the first time she had been there, to get her cards after starting work at the Duchamps', she had been turned away at the counter and thought, enemy aliens *sind hier unerwünscht*: like the Jews in Germany; she was merely being sent across the yard to the juvenile section but the emotions which she had had then still clung to the place. Her parents believed that she was still at school: by now her letters to them were filled from beginning to end with if not lies then truths dressed up; sometimes she thought that she hoped for Dolph's release merely so that she would no longer have to write to them.

Another domestic post? the girl behind the desk asked her and started looking through her files. Inge reminded herself who she was and said, no: she was looking for something better. "But what else are you good for?" the girl asked her. Inge fled.

The following Thursday, the Doctor, seeing her high colour at breakfast time, asked her, gruffly, "Got a date, have you?" and she felt tempted to confess to him what she was up to. But supposing he begged her, for his sake, to stay on? She believed that the occasional sixpence he slipped her, saying that it was for working overtime, was a bribe to make her put up with his wife: they usually came after she had been screamed at. He, too, wasn't Atlas; lines which she was sure had not been there before had joined the others about his eyes, his mouth, and he was so preoccupied when he got up in the morning that he sometimes forgot to change his underpants. Just to do some little extra thing for him—before she left—she decided that in future she would clean his shoes.

Please God let there be some other girl, she prayed as she reached the labour exchange; thus she had prayed in her desperate childhood, please God don't let the teacher be a Nazi. The same girl was there; but there was a second desk which offered her the choice of a motherly-looking woman. Would Inge like to become a hairdresser? It would be useful to her after the war, to have a trade! Inge stopped herself only just in time from telling her, that's not what I left my home for; she doubted if hairdressers would be wanted in a kibbutz. But she took the card she was given, and another which entitled her to apply at a grocer's for the job of errand-girl.

The grocer told her that she would need to be able to ride a bicycle, as if he believed that they were unknown where she came from, and then scratched his head and said, "My customers wouldn't like it," meaning the vestige of her German accent, which she had held on to in spite of Miss Pym as part of her identity. She believed that she had got the job at the hairdresser's but nothing came of it.

She tried again the next week, and the next; the thought of making a home for Dolph drove her on.

One day she was cleaning the china displayed on the upper shelves—it meant carrying it down the step-ladder, and up again; she had been told to do it so that his household would not shame the Doctor when he put up the Christmas decorations; she thought that if he had been asked he might have judged it better to spare her the ordeal. But she was fairly cheerful about it, assuming that it meant that Sebastian was expected home: they would hardly be putting up Christmas decorations for themselves. She had spent much thought on what to give him: it must not be something he could have bought for himself; she bought a leather-bound notebook—the size of Dolph's Heine which Rudi had said was just right for the trenches—to be filled with her favourite poems. She was wondering whether or not to include Thomas Hood's *The Bridge of Sighs*; the theme of the girl of whom no one knew anything appealed to her, and especially the stanza,

> Alas! for the rarity
> Of Christian charity
>   Under the sun!
> O, it was pitiful!
> Near a whole city full,
>   Home she had none.

She wanted him to read this; but the poem was very long and very sorrowful and she had understood that Sebastian, as if he were a refugee, also needed sustaining. Her mind thus not being on her work, she dropped an antique tureen.

The crash of it brought Mrs Duchamp into the kitchen. "Sabotage!" she screamed. "Don't think it will do you any good! You will pay for it out of your wages!" Though if she had gone on working for nothing for a year it would not have paid for it. "Here you are and here you'll stay!" Mrs Duchamp screamed, and Inge wondered what time it was; a wristwatch was one of the things other—English—people had; she thought that Mrs Duchamp meant, here on top of the ladder, until the Doctor came home.

Whenever Mrs Duchamp began to scream, Inge shut off her

hearing; about one word in ten got through and one caught her attention: Mrs Duchamp was telling her that the woman in the labour exchange was a friend of hers, and every time Inge applied for a job Mrs Duchamp rang her prospective employers to tell them that Inge was a liar and a thief and an enemy alien.

When she was left alone, sitting on top of the step-ladder, crying, her thoughts from life-long habit turned to Dolph though he was not the consolation he used to be. It was not he who needed a home, he had written: once released he had no intention of staying in England, where nothing was going on— she thought that perhaps he meant that like some of Rudi's relations he would go to some neutral country to escape the war, he had mentioned Switzerland as a first step. In his opinion, he had written in a letter which had for once taken only a week to reach her, it did not matter if she had to stay with the Duchamps a little longer—he meant to ease the pressure on her but she misread this as indifference; at least she would be sure of getting a Christmas dinner even if she did have to eat it by herself in the kitchen. She thought back to the Christmasses of their child-hood, when they had looked through the windows of other people's houses at their beautiful trees, and envied them the possession of little Georgies—they hadn't been Georgies then—adorable in their mangers; they had walked, cold hand in cold hand, through the snow-transfigured streets lit up—as if the town itself were a Christmas tree—by the shop-windows full of goodies which were always only for others and not for them.

It gave her an idea.

She got down from her perch, and out of habit absent-mindedly swept up the sherds, and, after her servant's lunch, as soon as Mrs Duchamp had gone out, also left the house, took the tram to the town centre and in the first shop she came to asked if they needed extra help because of the Christmas shoppers. It was a jeweller's and she realized her mistake at once: her aim would have to be more in keeping with her station. She tried a dress-shop and a shoe-shop—but she could not bear the thought of sitting at people's feet; by the time she had tried half a dozen shops she had perfected a story to anticipate their questions: she had come from London to get away from the bombs, her father and mother and two sisters had been killed in an air-raid—she could not manage these interviews without crying; she would not say that her brother had been killed; she explained that she had not had much practical experience, had of course still been at school, but her father had had a shop—of whatever type she happened to have walked into; no, not in London of course, in Berlin. They had owned Wertheim's, she felt like saying, to give herself backbone, but decided to keep her lies decent.

It worked.

After she had been engaged as a junior in the dress department of just such a department store, she took the tram to the Jewish neighbourhood where refugees were reassured, and started to look for a home. She had imagined taking a flat but found that on her wages—and how was she to go on paying the rent after Christmas?—she could not afford even two rooms: one for Dolph. "But you must go to your relations!" she was told, and when she said that she had none to go to was told that that could not possibly be true. She was told that she was too young to think of living in a bed-sitter on her own. She was turned away because she would have been too much responsibility. Refugee householders expected her, one to share a bed with their six-year-old daughter, another to sleep on a couch in their living-room, reminding her, "Whatever happens to us here in England, we are the lucky ones!" One elderly widow would have taken her in, promising to treat her like a daughter—and Inge fled, unable to bear the thought of starting all over again.

It was beginning to get dark and Mrs Duchamp would have got home by now and found her out—she could not enjoy the pun; all the euphoria of landing another job had been walked off. She could not face going back and had nowhere else to go; wildly she thought, when she passed a group of men who looked at her merely because she was passing, that surely even a refugee could become a prostitute—and have a bed. With pains in her knees—her shoes needed re-heeling—she wandered about; if she had come to water, she thought, she would have thrown herself in, like the girl in *The Bridge of Sighs*. She recited the poem to herself; it was no comfort. She started thinking one up—which served to make her, through love of the English language, forget her circumstances.

In the end she went to the Doctor's surgery; it was still crowded and she sat in a corner, in a daze, as far withdrawn from life as she could be without sleeping; she almost missed him. The receptionist, turning the lights out, found her and ran after the Doctor, already getting into his car; he had left by the surgery door. He came back and when Inge saw his caring face she burst into tears.

She wept because she had thought that what had been wrong with her life until now was that she had simply allowed things to happen to her, and she had thought of doing something about it as making it better. But what was better about an existence without the Doctor's daily presence, without the constant expectation of Sebastian, what the hell was the matter with her that she could not get along with his mother, who had created within her the beginnings of this perfect young man? The Doctor was saying that it was time for her to leave them, if she did not want to become a part of their family; perhaps he had meant, she decided when she thought it over afterwards, that she would have become one of those old-fashioned retainers, who serve generation after generation, until they are pensioned off by one whom they rocked in his cradle. At the time, her attention was absorbed altogether by the first part of that sentence, which sounded to her as if even the Doctor would be glad to be rid of her. It would be wiser—more adult, more English—she decided, to do the rejecting before being rejected; therefore, as the Doctor drove her home—the abuse of words! she thought, but what else was she to call the only address she had?—she agreed that she ought not to work out her week's notice, for the sake of his peace.

The next day, after she had finished her chores, she went forth again, and had no trouble finding herself a room: in the frame of mind of wanting to get away renting an attic at which she would have turned her nose up the day before, when she still had illusions—more illusions—about what was to become of her. The Doctor transported her suitcase, and slipped her a couple of pound notes—her Christmas bonus, he called it—and told her to keep in touch; it was to be nine months before they met again.

That very evening she sent her new address to her brother, to Rudi, to Hansi, to Jean Crowther, and—as an excuse for writing to him—to Sebastian; gratified that there were now so many people in her life she also sent it to Hamish, Hansi's half-brother. Hansi had told her that, in the last war, her father had been in Scotland as a prisoner, working on the land, and when he had been repatriated he had left behind him a son: he had been Hansi's guarantor. Inge had been so busy listening to Hansi that she had only half heard what she was being told, and believed that it was the half-brother who had been a German soldier; she thought of him, when she wrote, as belonging to her parents' generation. Hansi had told her that he was running a babies' home, not far from Glasgow; Inge thought it an odd occupation for a man, and assumed that he was too old to be doing something to help the war effort. His answer was short though kind: if she should ever find herself north of the border she should look him up, he was always good for a bed and perhaps a job as well; to Inge this—from a half-German to a Jew—sounded patronizing; she was unimpressed by his handwriting, as artless as Hansi's was flamboyant, and by the cheap notepaper on which something—milk?—had been spilled: she thought that he ought not to have sent it to her like that. But she copied his address into the little book she had bought, for the sake not of having it but of filling another space; it was some months before she wrote to him again.

She liked her new job, especially the going into the store by an almost secret entrance before it opened its public doors, and taking the dust-sheets off as if she were in charge, and being there without a coat on as if she owned the place, and going behind the scenes as if she belonged.

She was less satisfied with her room, in which she was cold: it had a slot-meter for the gas which she nicknamed Hitler because she did what she could to appease it and it was never enough for long. She had a dormer window which was nailed shut and overlooked the rooftops, and a leaking skylight; the light bulb was weak and in the wrong place for reading in bed, which she did to keep warm; it did not occur to her to smuggle a stronger bulb in, or that she could have moved the bed. That winter she got again the chilblains of her childhood, not altogether unwelcome with their echoes of home, especially when they only half woke her in the night. She had a gas-ring, which she could not use at the same time as the fire; she could not be bothered to cook for herself but lived on tea-cakes and, as long as the ration lasted, cheese; the tea-cakes worked out cheaper than bread, which went stale before she could finish a loaf, and helped to satisfy her craving for sweet things. Somehow she never managed to register with the milkman; tea without milk no longer tasted right to her and instead she drank soup made out of Oxo cubes. By the spring, she had got rather thin—slender, she called it to herself, rhyming it with "sent her" and "defend her"; even her little titties threatened to desert her.

Now there remained to her only two things which she had brought with her from home. Her camera had been packed, for safe-keeping, in Miss Pym's luggage, and she had not bothered to ask her to send it on, partly because she did not want to be threatened with hell-fire and partly because she believed that on her sixteenth birthday she would anyway have to give it up; Dolph's camera had been confiscated long ago by the East Lothian police. The straw hat she had got for going to Palestine with, Miss Pym had judged suitable holiday wear in the convent guest-house; she had forgotten that its crown was stuffed with a red and white dirndl—Rudi would call it a Freudian forgetting because it brought with it an image of her mother standing ironing it. On the evening on which she sewed tucks into her black salesgirl's dress, she decided to try it on, and when she found that it fitted her grew euphoric: as if it meant that she was also still the same girl within, the one her parents had cherished. She put on her magical straw hat and, translated into a pioneer with a right to the Promised Land, danced about her English attic wishing that Dolph could see her.

She would not have liked it if she had been living in a place where no one took notice of her comings and goings, where none would have paid attention if she had not got up in the morning so that if she were to fall ill she would be left lying untended until she died, or where she would not be missed if she were knocked down in the blackout so that she would be left to lie unclaimed in a hospital or a morgue, while Dolph, and Sebastian, and Rudi, and Hansi and Jean Crowther, to say nothing of her parents, would wonder why she no longer wrote to them. Her landlady, a tiny old woman, on letting the attic to her had asked her, "Are you a good girl?" and she had been tempted to answer, if I weren't would I tell you? (When, after Christmas, the personnel manager of the store had told her that it had been decided to keep her on, he called her a good girl— which she resented almost as much as being called a funny one, again without knowing why.)

The landlady obviously did not trust her: snooped about among her things; once she confronted Inge with one of her poems—she was still occasionally writing in German—and, indicating the indentation of some lines—on the pattern of Hood's *Bridge of Sighs*—asked her, was this not some sort of code? All that paper Jill had in her room, she said: if Jill would not throw it out she would do it for her: she was the one whose responsibility it was to see that there was no undue fire hazard—this was the spring of the blitz. It was because she wanted somewhere to store her manuscripts that Inge wrote again to Hansi's half-brother Hamish: his was the only address she knew which was both permanent and safe—apart from Sebastian's which she did not want to make use of because many of her early poems had been sparked off by Rudi and it would be just like her luck if one of these were to fall out and make him discover her inconstancy.

When Hamish agreed to store whatever she sent him, she felt that politeness demanded that she should tell him that he could read what he wished; still mistaking him for a middle-aged ex-POW, she did not think that his judgement would matter to her. She was astonished that he should have bothered, when he wrote back, quite soon, that he had read everything, including what she had written in German; would she let him know whether or not she would like him to make some comments: he would tread softly since he was treading on her dreams. Recognizing the quotation from Yeats, at that time her soul-mate, she was intrigued, and told herself that she ought to have known that even a half-brother of Hansi's would be somebody worth having as a correspondent. She wrote to Hansi asking, did he have her green eyes and auburn hair or—she was learning to vault across embarrassments by means of a joke, like the English—was he perhaps bald? He became the new father-figure in her life, the Doctor's replacement. Hansi wrote back,

His hair is black and his eyes are blue
And I would love him if I were you!

Inge was hugely offended; she was beginning to wonder if Hansi
was really as marvellous as she had at first thought: or would
she be worshipping their Dolph-David quite so uncritically?

One May evening, when she came home, having had enough for
the day of the English world and looking forward to being
herself and alone, her little old landlady waylaid her to tell her
that she had had a caller; her first visitor. "An airforce officer?"
she asked, feeling as if the woman had grabbed hold not of her
sleeve but her heart; Rudi had been catastrophically wrong, or
else she did not matter to Sebastian more than a little: in five
months they had exchanged a dozen or so letters but he had not
sought her out. She did not blame him; she did not blame Rudi
for overestimating her, though she thought less of him for it.

"He's no officer," the crone said. "And no gentleman neither I
shouldn't wonder." Not, then, even Rudi, Inge had already
decided by the time she added, "Foreign-spoken, like."
Definitely not Rudi, whose English had long been true-blue. She
had sent him away "with a flea in his ear"—an expression
which, at another time, would have made Inge want to hug her.
The crone took her hand to steady herself as she stood on tiptoe
to peer, in the dim light of the hall, into her face. "He tried to get
into your room by claiming to be your brother."

It felt to Inge as if her heart, from being a pupa, had hatched
out as a butterfly. "Do you have a brother?" the crone was
asking her.

She thinks he's a fifth columnist, Inge thought, her carapace
doing credit to all her mentors in England; within it, the Jewish
refugee brew steamed and stank as it bubbled up to the boil.
"Yes," she answered as Peter ought to have done when the cock
crowed. "Oh yes, I have a brother." Who, unlike Sebastian,
unlike Rudi even, did not look like a gentleman and spoke only
broken English—she was soon to wish that that were all that
was wrong with him.

The old Dolph would have planted himself on the door step
and not budged; she remembered finding him, at the Sparrows,

among the milk bottles—so that he was in her mind as the gipsy urchin he had looked then, twenty-one months ago, when she saw him again, and she thought him even more changed than he was.

She had not known that he shaved and he had grown a moustache; the skin about his eyes was creased and folded as if his skull had shrunk; he kept his eyes in hiding with constant blinking and by tilting his head; he was wearing a—quite good—light grey tweed suit a size too small; the colour was wrong for him, made him appear more haggard; he looked dissolute, in need of a bath and bed.

"You look terrible," were the first words he said to her, after twenty-one months.

"Close your eyes," she commanded as if she were the elder one; they came together in a long, blind embrace. But he felt more substantial and smelled of manhood. "When did you get out?" she asked with her mouth in his smoky hair.

"A week, ten days ago," he answered as if it hardly mattered, and she disengaged herself: all the hurts sustained through him in her childhood did not, together, amount to as much. Sensing it, he explained, "I stayed on in Liverpool because of the bombing." Thus he used to say, I stayed on after school because of the football. Not knowing that he had wanted to test his nerve, and had helped to dig through the ruins, she was appalled by him.

"Can I come in?" he asked, lightly: to remind her that they were still standing on the doorstep under the hostile eye of the landlady; she stopped them from going upstairs together. "He is my brother!" Inge exclaimed; the words made it true and he was, come the Flood or Judgement Day. She clutched hold of him, who was part of her, as if pinching herself to check that she was not dreaming. "Well then, take him into the parlour," the landlady said, opening the door to it for them and switching the light on. "Who needs privacy with a brother?" The room was permanently blacked-out and rarely used: it smelled unaired and was chilly. "The young man may light the gas-fire for us," the landlady said. But, like Hitler, it required to have its demands met at once. "I haven't any money," Dolph said, unembarrassed, grinning his boyhood grin; he did not explain then that

123

he had given it all away, to those in more need of it—with not a thought for his mendacious sister.

She went to fetch some. Later that night, undressing for bed, she found bruises on her thighs and wondered how they had got there: she had been belabouring them with her fists as if she were beating drums to summon help, on the long climb up to her attic, thinking, what am I going to do with him, what am I going to do?

She was used to coming down those stairs always only reluctantly. Returning braced for an ordeal and confronted with her brother—her brother!—she could ignore to what extent he had changed. All that mattered was what still made him familiar. "Dolph! Dolph!" she said, at his elbow while he lit the fire. When he straightened up, he looked at her, but not as if she were the sight his eyes had craved for; he said again, "You look terrible."

Inge thought, I could say the same; if she had learned anything from Sebastian it was that one must behave better than other people in order to keep one's self-respect. She smiled at her brother and he asked, "Why are you wearing mourning?" but did not wait for her to finish explaining that all the assistants in the store wore plain black and that she preferred it to her white-frilled housemaid's uniform. "What's that on your face?" he asked as if he did not know that girls used make-up; Hansi had worn lipstick; Inge wore more than that: she had to: all the people in the dress department had told her that without it the strip lighting under which they worked made her look like a ghost. Dolph was still doing his reconnaissance of her. "What have you done to your hair?" Mrs Duchamp had liked her to keep it plaited to stop it from getting into the soup; but in public Inge could not wear plaits which she considered German; since the store would not allow her to wear it loose she had had it cut to shoulder-length and was nightly putting it into curlers though it did not need it; the other junior in her department had told her that this was the smart thing to do and shown her how to do it.

He wanted to have her weeping in his arms, not only because it would have comforted him, and was trying to break down her self-control: thought it unnatural, unhealthy, could tell by the way she was holding herself how much it cost her. He took her hands and without looking, by the familiar feel of them, discovered her chilblains. "Oh, Inge!" he exclaimed, his voice thick with, she thought, reproach. "Can't you do something about them?" It was meant as a question but came out as a criticism. He ran his hands up her arms. "Do you have to be so thin?" He meant, are you ill? but could not manage those words. In his mind, he saluted all her brave lies while cursing himself for failing to read the signals; he was appalled by this evidence of how much she still needed him. Seeing her half-starved reminded him that he was hungry.

Inge was hungry too; she had been busy setting out what food she had in her attic when the landlady had called her to the street door. "I'll bring it down," she said readily, but paused to comfort her palms on his shaggy hair.

While she was upstairs, the landlady went into her kitchen but, wanting to keep an eye on the visitor, let her milk boil over; Inge could smell it as she came back and Dolph greeted her with, "Do you think she'd let me have some?" like a small boy; he was the only person she had ever come across to whom the skin on boiled milk was a delicacy. "It brings it all back," he said and Inge, thinking that no one except she—not even Hansi!—knew all it brought back for him, felt herself flooding with love, drowning in it; she said, "Like Proust's madeleine." She could see that he did not know what she was talking about. He was concentrating on getting as much butter as he could—four days' ration—on to the tea-cake; he finished what cheese she had in two bites, while she was thinking, I am better educated than he is, I know more than he does, he hasn't had my advantages. Her one knife and one plate had misled him into believing that she had already eaten and she let them: getting more satisfaction out of the sight of her rations going into the making of Dolph.

"Is that all there is?" he asked her. "Then let's go out for a meal!" He put his hands in his pockets, remembered that he was broke, and said, "You'll have to lend me some money." He saw the consternation on her face and watched it for a moment before asking, gently, "You must have some?"

She did not want him to think her incompetent, useless; she had never lied to him—only to his address—and she could not lie to him now that he seemed to have lost all his Dolphish attributes. "I have seventeen shillings and sixpence," she told him. "I'm saving up for a pair of shoes," and offered him a foot to let him see for himself that it was necessary. "Get it," he commanded, and when she hesitated told her, "It's a loan, Ingele, I'll give it back to you!" She did not believe him but off she went, to exchange her savings for a few minutes away from him from whom she had never before in all her life wanted to escape.

As they were leaving the house—it was just beginning to get dark—he said, quite cheerfully, "As you can't put me up I'd better start off for London straight away." It got him a gut-melting look and he put an arm about her shoulders and explained, "After we've eaten, after I've seen you home. There are some people I've got to talk to, I came here first because I couldn't wait to see you." He knew what it felt like to her, as if she were a dog being wagged by its tail, because he occasionally got the same feeling. He said, "I'll be back. I want to see something of you before I go."—"Go where?" she asked, while he was saying, "In the meantime, see if you can find me some work, anything, so long as it's well-paid." Not until then had she realised that "internment" was a euphemism for imprisonment. He was a released *prisoner*. She must not blame him: how was he to know what wartime England was like, that he must register with the police and get their permission to come or to stay or to go, must register with the labour exchange and get permission from them too, and that not all jobs were open to enemy aliens and that not many which were were well-paid? He probably believed that, having served his sentence, he was now a free man.

He was asking, "How much do you need to see you through?"—"Through what?" she asked and when he did not answer, told him, "I get twenty-five shillings, less the stamps and the five shillings for the staff lunches, and I pay nine shillings a week rent and—"

"Two hundred pounds should do it," he interrupted her, meaning: supplement what she could earn until she was old enough to be paid a living wage or get married or if the war were not over by then join Hansi in the ATS. "I ought to be able to lay my hands on that," he said as if he were planning to rob a bank;

she thought that, of course, he had no idea of the value of English money.

She was making for the tea-shop in which Mrs Duchamp and her friends liked to be seen in their WVS uniforms—as if the feeling of belonging which she got from being with her brother had misled her into believing that she now had the freedom of the city. The place was closed. Further down the road, they could have got fish and chips; she had reached the stage where this was a treat but Dolph turned his nose up at it: he did not want her to grow old remembering their reunion against the background of a fish and chip shop. He asked, "Don't you know of anywhere better? You have been in Leeds for how long?" She never ate out, she had told him before she remembered eating out with Sebastian.

In the early days of her independence as a shop-assistant she had haunted the approaches to the place in the hope of encountering him as if accidentally, but when it had happened he had been the hub of a group of friends, walking backwards and turning to give them all equally the benefit of his attention and she had first hid from him and then run away from herself, and from then on had thought it wiser to take her daydreams to the cinema, where at least she would not be misled into believing that they might come true.

The spurious confidence generated by her brother's presence carried her beyond the outer, makeshift entrance which was there because of the blackout; but her courage failed her when she could see him again: in the charity suit—just like in Germany—which he had been given because the rescue work had spoiled the one in which he had been released from the Isle of Man; what luggage he had had with him had been lost in a raid or stolen; most of his belongings, packed by Hansi, were still stored somewhere in Scotland. She hung back, saying, "It's much too good for us!" though later she argued that what she had meant was, too expensive. Dolph gave her a blood-curdling look of scorn: because after two years and five months in England she had still not grown out of thinking of herself as a victim. He went up to the doorkeeper and came back saying, "First we're bloody Jews and now we're bloody refugees!" It was meant as sarcasm but she looked so stricken that he kissed her and explained, "It's an airforce club, little idiot! Now what? This is your city." To be told this would under other circumstances have made her sparkle; but now she was mortified to find that life was no better with him beside her than it had been without him. His tell-tale charity tweeds were cobwebbed with rain.

An airman looked at them in passing and came back, having recognized her as Bill's schoolgirl who liked blue films. "Does Bill know that you're waiting?" She almost crawled behind Dolph, her shield against strangers for longer than she could remember; she heard the man's "Hey, Bill!" and there he was: more Sebastian than ever, the ideal Aryan in the choicest blue.

He seemed to be delighted to see her; since she could not believe that he was and saw no reason why he should pretend to be, she believed that she was only imagining it or that, perhaps, he was delighted that she had got her brother back or delighted with her brother: quickly—too quickly for her—he turned to shake hands with him. "How do you do," he said and Dolph, like a stage refugee, answered, "I do oi veh so bad with my hot cock in the bathroom!" For the first time in all her life Inge was ashamed of him.

But Sebastian grinned at him, encouragingly; his look swivelled between brother and sister as if, Inge thought, he were choosing between them; he chose Dolph: put a protective arm about his shoulders—because he should not have had to laugh at himself before others could laugh at him, he was to tell her— and steered him through the door, his other hand holding her by the sleeve to draw her in their wake. The hall was crowded and warm, fuggy with cigarette smoke, and noisy. Sebastian pulled a chair out for Inge and as he pushed it in under her, put his mouth close to her ear and whispered, "What's the matter with him?"

Inge, who had not known that there was anything the matter, answered with conviction and sulks, "He's hungry." From somewhere—a passing waiter or another table—Sebastian conjured up a plate of anchovies on toast to put before Dolph at once. To make it plain that they were there as his guests, he ordered their food without even consulting them. He had already eaten; he had a whisky, but did not drink it: as if he could get all the sustenance he needed from watching Dolph eating and from listening to his cataract of words, so badly pronounced that it did not sound like English.

Inge had the impression that they were attracting attention and perhaps they were: in that place, where people were known if not to each other then to each other's friends, a young man in civvies was a rarity; perhaps they found it intriguing that Bill's girl had turned up with another boy, and such a one.

You could see every mouthful of food doing him good; in those surroundings, under Sebastian's gaze, his smouldering eyes took on a bonfire look; thus had his cheeks used to look chafed in boyhood when he had been mastering some new skill, roller-skating, say, or chess-playing. He was explaining to Sebastian that the fabulous gift he had for learning languages was of no practical use to him because he had no ear. While he had been learning Turkish, and modern Greek, and Walloon, and Flemish, there had been no one to question his pronunciation; he had believed that his accent in English was due to his living cut off from native English-speakers; only having an Italian girlfriend had brought his handicap incontrovertibly home to him. Even in Germany he would not be able to pass for other than a Westphalian.

He kept glancing at Inge, to find reassurance or fault she could not tell; he was keeping an eye on her because he was talking chiefly for her benefit; he could not tell her to her face, I am going to try and rescue Mutti and Papa—in case he failed. Seeing her so aghast, he believed her to be listening, while she was paying so much attention to the sound of what he was saying that she did not take in more than a word here and there; what upset her were his bad table-manners, his un-English loquacity. Sebastian, she could see, was captivated by him, as Rudi had once been she thought in her ignorance; what was true was that he was again just as much in need of an instant friend. Their mother had used to say of him that he was able to charm a horse out from under its rider. Sebastian was patting his arm and saying, "But David, you can't go back to Germany." Inge thought that they must be talking about after the war. "Take it easy and look around—you are how old?"

Dolph put his knife and fork down, his appetite suddenly

gone. He hid the trembling of his hands under the table but that left one only the more aware of his spectacular face. "Do you mean," he began with his voice reined in, "that I have all the time in the world to do this?" Inge could see that Sebastian had not meant that though she did not understand that what he was baulking at was that Dolph should risk his life before he had ever—in Sebastian's view—had the chance to enjoy it. As red as turkey-wattles, Dolph continued, "You English are all the same, you have no sense of urgency, no wonder you don't show any signs of winning the war!" He ended up shouting, and everybody had listened: he had meant them to hear him. Inge wished that the trout on her plate were a whale that would swallow her up. People were waiting to be shown by their Bill, their old man—his host—how to react; Sebastian put his head in his hands and groaned, "Oh, my God!" and looked up and told him, "You've a right to be angry with me, I hadn't at all understood what we've done by interning you." Inge believed that he meant, ruined his manners; he would remember that she knew how to behave and not blame their parents. Sebastian, looking at Dolph as if he were Fletcher Christian, was saying, "I'm your man, Dave, you can count on me, Dave, I'm your man!" Dolph turned to Inge and asked her, "You don't mind if I make use of your boyfriend?" He knew very well that he was not that and was trying to be helpful to Sebastian.

Oh, the shame, Inge thought, of having Sebastian believe that she had so misrepresented their relationship! Sebastian gave her a smile; feeling that she had come by it dishonestly, she did not begin to cherish it until afterwards.

Dolph said to him, "Some of your chaps have passed through there, tell me what conditions are like for them." Sebastian stood up, and after looking round sat down again and said something to their neighbours; Inge could hear the message, being passed on, turn into, "Bobby Roberts, our old man wants you!"

An airman came to the table and Sebastian asked him, "Where did you come down?" He answered, "Just south of Lübeck." Brother and sister looked at each other: it was not all that far from their home town; the name was familiar to them from one of their favourite ballads. "Tell Dave about it and don't keep anything back," Sebastian told him, making room for him next to Dolph, and turned to Inge.

She did not believe that the warmth of his look was for her: he had merely forgotten, as Rudi had sometimes done, to turn down the flame. It mortified her to discover that she was jealous of her brother, as she had not been in the days of Rudi—she had yet to learn that then she had had more cause; she thought not that it was because she was sexually ripening but—with her brother's example before her—because being a refugee corroded the character. As if to prove it she asked, belligerently, "Why haven't you ever asked me to meet you?"

Sebastian was half-listening to the conversation at his back; it was a moment before he answered, "I thought that you preferred letters to live encounters. Because," he raised his eyebrows at her like a schoolmaster, "you will still have them tomorrow." She had once told him that she tried to spend her money in such a way that it would leave her with something to show for it tomorrow; she was astonished that he should remember it. He was trying to tease her and she believed that he was making fun of her.

Into their silence, she heard her brother saying, "One is handicapped by varicose veins and the other has a bad heart," and thought, that sounds as if he were talking of Mutti and Papa, and thought, with real anguish—Rudi was right to say that she had no sense of proportion—oh, why can't he know how people behave in England! He had his elbows on the table and was rubbing his eyes with his fists.

At least partly so as to distract Sebastian, she told him, shakily, "I don't, you know," and had to explain that she meant that she didn't prefer letters. As if Dolph were infectious, he also ceased to know how to behave: leaned forward and whispered into her ear, "I'm a coward," and sat back as if he had never moved. Eventually—days later—she decided that he must have meant that he was afraid of having her mistaken for his girlfriend.

When the escaper's girl came up to remind him that they were meant to go dancing, he asked Dolph, "Would you like to go dancing, Dave?" and Sebastian instantly asked Inge, "Would you like to go dancing, Jill?" Brother and sister sought each other's eyes: they had never been inside a ballroom, had never danced anything except the *horrah*; Dolph was to tell her that he had felt like a midget mistaken for one of the children. She saw him needing her help and nothing mattered as much, not even becoming Sebastian's Cinderella. "There's a curfew for us," she reminded them all, though it would not apply to her for another few months when she would be sixteen; she did not mind being an enemy alien when it made her and her brother a pair.

To hell with the curfew, Sebastian said, it did not matter while they were with him. Dolph said something about hitchhiking to London and Sebastian, as Rudi had once done, assumed the rights of an elder brother. To hell with the war for one night: the morning train would get him there as quickly, and to hell with money. As if he were after all drunk he suddenly shouted, with a hand on Dolph's shoulder so that all should know who was meant, "He says that he needs a bed to sleep in!" Inge gathered that this was a joke. To hell with sleeping, the others agreed with their Bill, their old man; but when someone called out, "The Jerries will have your balls soon enough!" Sebastian as suddenly sobered up and, as if he belonged to an older generation or as if they were mortally ill, shepherded brother and sister out and demanded a taxi.

He decided that they should take Inge home first. She had already got out when Dolph remembered her seventeen shillings and sixpence and gave it back to her. Sebastian—presumably because he did not know that it was hers—got out his wallet also to give her some money, but she would not accept it. He handed it to Dolph, who offered it to her, saying, "You may take it, it's mine, he gave it to me." Oh the unfairness of it! she thought, getting no pleasure at all out of her sudden wealth, and meaning not only that he would be a guest in the house where she had been a servant but that being a girl precluded her from such instant uncomplicated comradeship, and that they needed each other more than either of them needed her.

The two young men went to a dance-hall, but only long enough to pick up a couple of women, a little older than Sebastian—who was not quite five years older than Dolph—who fought a private war not over the squadron-leader but over the smouldering youngster. They went to the home of one of them and afterwards the young men returned to the airforce club, Sebastian to get drunk and Dolph to watch over him; to create for himself a situation in which he was no longer in control went against the grain with him.

Sebastian, when he had reached the maudlin stage, produced the photographs he carried in his wallet, demanding of David that he should do the same: were they not each other's best pals? The only photograph he carried was that of his sister, Dolph told him. Sebastian proposed that they should trade: let Dolph take his pick! Dolph said that he did not want to have his sister's face among the faces of Sebastian's tarts. Sebastian told him that in exchange he could have them all and when Dolph refused them, made the round of other drinkers, trying to give them away. When no one would take them he went back to his table and ceremoniously burned them in an ashtray. Dolph let him pocket Inge's photograph, thinking that it would serve to remind him to keep an eye on her.

His letters from London were full of impatience, frustration, rage. The English did not know and refused to be told that it was a matter of life and death; they kept telling him that the Jews in Germany were not the only people who were threatened, that the priority must be to rid the world of Hitler. That he was not yet eighteen, as if he did not know his own age. That he would do best to wait until he could join the Commandos—if the small matter of his nationality could be overcome. He had had great hopes of the Free French and the Poles but they were interested only in their own. If only he could think of a way of making himself dumb, short of cutting his tongue out, he would be able to pass himself off as belonging to any nationality, he could learn to understand any bloody language he chose. If only their great-great-great-grandfathers had remained Polish! If he had had any other passport the English would have let him do anything, would have been only too happy to have him parachute into Germany to blow up a railway. As it was, they kept telling him that he was doing himself no good by being so pushing, that he was being too emotional, that he ought not to expect special treatment— when all he wanted was to be allowed to do this one thing and then they could have him. To Inge, it sounded like raving.

He was staying with Jean Crowther, he wrote, whose idea of mothering was to try to talk him out of doing what he most wanted to do—but he and she (Inge) knew that a real Mutti was not like that. He wished all the world were like Inge: not a word of encouragement because she knew that he did not need it, not a word to hold him back because she was not so selfish. Since he assumed that she knew what he was wanting to do she assumed that she knew it too. He had never before allowed her to take such an intimate interest in his every move, she could not understand why he wrote to her almost every day—wasting a fortune on postage—mostly brief scrawls on grubby paper—as if he did not have time to wash his hands; she threw some away before she realized that she must be meant to keep them, as a sort of record, for their children or perhaps for Joachim Meyer's parents.

Then came a happier letter, saying that Hansi had wangled some leave to see if she could help him and even if she couldn't having her with him did him good, perhaps one day . . . Inge's estimation of Hansi went up like a barrage balloon, because Dolph expected her to be able to accomplish what he could not. Imagine her, he wrote, striding through the establishments of the Establishment, giving apoplexy to the colonels; her manner even more than her looks opened all doors to her—in rather than out of the colonels' offices; Inge gathered that by colonels he meant the authorities but failed to understand what else he meant. Sebastian too, he wrote, believed in going straight to the top and had provided him with an introduction to an air-vice-marshal; Inge had not known that Sebastian had remained in touch: phoned him every couple of days or so, drunk or sober and sometimes in the middle of the night, to enquire how he was getting on and to give him the chance to discuss it with someone who understood him.

In the middle of July, suddenly, things began to run on wheels for him. Somebody mentioned him to Chaim Weizmann, who asked to see him. Dolph wrote that they talked alone together for more than two hours and that what Weizmann had told him on parting had been very helpful. Inge believed that he was making it up—or why did he not repeat to her what the great man had said? He had been put in touch with Aunt Ruchamah, he wrote—it was years before Inge learned that this was the name of one of the rescue organizations. Aunt Ruchamah was going to substitute him for one of her regular couriers, to get him by air to Lisbon and, with luck, perhaps even as far as Switzerland; from there he would be on his own.

If Inge did not have a recent photograph she must have one taken at once; she must have one taken in any case, like this: wearing a roll-neck jumper to hide her salt-cellars and with her hair forward over her cheeks to disguise that she was so thin; she must on no account wear her Star of David, and not curl her hair the night before (deferring to him, she had already stopped doing it; she had stopped using make-up, even in the store: the only approval that mattered to her was her brother's). No doubt he would be asked when it had been taken—Inge wondered by whom—so it had to be up-to-date. He would come to fetch it.

He was a hurricane force and she was his still centre. Success or rather absence of frustration had changed him; he looked, Inge thought, like Aunt Ruchamah's favourite nephew, and not only because Jean Crowther had treated him to a new suit. He had brought her £200: a gift from someone who thought that he ought at least not to have to worry about his little sister while he was on his mission; to Aunt Ruchamah such a sum must have been petty cash and perhaps part of it was his pay and/or what he meant to save on expenses; or it may have come from Dr Duchamp, who knew through Sebastian what Jill's brother was up to. To Inge, it meant disappointment: he would not be staying in Leeds for any length of time as he had, she believed, promised; just as well that, remembering the Russian grammar, she had not even tried to find him work. His mention of smuggling something (false passports?) into Switzerland, coupled with some pre-war tins of food that he had brought—pheasant in aspic and turtle soup—which were a present to her from Jean Crowther, made her believe that he had got himself mixed up in the black market.

She was not altogether certain that she still liked him: he had become cagey and bossy. He made her take what holidays were due to her so that they could be together—they spent three days looking for somewhere else for her to live. She wanted a flat, no matter how small, so that she would be able to shut out the English world and do as she pleased and feel at home; she argued that she would rather spend her money—if it was hers to spend—on that than on anything else. But he did not want her to live alone, and used all the arguments, the same words almost, which she had used to reconcile herself to her nosy old landlady; therefore what else could she do but as always give in to him? They found a fine bay-fronted room on the top floor of a block of flats, overlooking a park. Inge objected to so many stairs: it would be she who would have to climb them every evening after being on her feet all day. Dolph told her that the view alone was worth it: rightly imagining that it would raise her spirits whenever she looked at it. The landlord's taste was not theirs but they did not find it objectionable and the place was clean. In such a room, Dolph told her, he would be able to entertain his friends—like Sebastian; it left Inge speechless: both the thought of being hostess to Sebastian and that Dolph had appropriated him. In addition they rented an attic, which would do for Dolph because he would not be there all the time—and if Hansi were ever to visit them there they could swop beds. "When!" she attempted to correct his English. "You only say if if it may never happen."—"When," he agreed, rewarding her with his most Dolphish grin: he believed that she was being heroic. They had the use of the kitchen but were expected to provide their own pots—Dolph insisted on buying more than one, so that she would be able to cook him proper meals—she should experiment and practise while she was on her own, he told her; he bought also a frying-pan, in case he wanted something to eat in a hurry. Trying to bluff her into having faith in his return, he was pretending that all they were doing was being done for him; she believed that camp life on the Isle of Man had made him utterly selfish. Even the child's teddy bear he bought, to replace the one lost to her on the Channel ferry, he claimed for his own, telling her that she could borrow it while he was away, knowing that this would enhance its value in her eyes.

Since they were not allowed to own a wireless, they bought a second-hand gramophone, and spent a happy afternoon browsing in a junk-shop through old records. That evening, while they were listening to songs of Schubert, she nerved herself to ask him, when he was winding the gramophone, "Why don't you marry Hansi?" He answered at once, without having to think about it, "Because if I don't come back, and she wants to marry again, it might be difficult for her to prove that I am dead." After a moment he added, "It makes no difference."

Unsure that she knew what he meant by that, she asked, "Do you . . . do you . . ." She did not know how to put it, in either language, without sounding offensive. Staying with English, she asked, "Do you remember: the birds are pecking?" Long ago, other children had told her to say it while pulling at the corners of her mouth with her little fingers; Dolph had had to explain the joke to her. "Sure we fuck," he now said with his atrocious accent and his nose in the air.

Inge asked, "What difference does it make, that you haven't a foreskin?" He explained that it made no difference when one had an erection. "Have I ever seen you with an erection?" she asked. He said that he supposed not. "I could show you," he offered, always the helpful brother; he was proud of his lusty cock. She was not interested in seeing a circumcised penis, she told him. Then she asked, "What does it do?"—"Don't you know?" he asked when he had got her to explain her question. "Hasn't anyone ever told you the facts of life?" Who should have told her? she asked back. "Mutti gave me a book to read before we left home, but I wasn't really interested, then, and it didn't bother me that I didn't understand it. It bothers me now. I don't even remember it, or not enough of it anyway."

"I'll get you a book before I leave," Dolph said, starting the gramophone up again. She had to raise her voice against it to beg him, "You tell me."

When he had come home, after his first day at school, with his cornucopia of sweets and his primer, asking what was the point of his going there when he happened already to know how to read and to write—it was a year before they had had to show him how to do one of his sums—his mother had said, "Go for the sake of telling Inge what it's like." He had had measles before her, so that when it came to her turn she already knew that she would have to lie in a darkened room, had had a sore throat so that she was prepared for having her tonsils squeezed and being sick. His birthday was a fortnight before hers, so that she was warned by the presents he received—fewer and smaller as the years went on—not to expect too much. She had always been his queen and he her cupbearer. He thought, her first encounter will make or mar her for life, and moved, so that he was not quite facing her but could keep a weather-eye on her reactions, as he stood in for their mother.

When he had finished, she thought it over for a while, then her hand went up to her ear. "Why start here?" she asked, fingering the lobe, glad now that her mother had not given in to her when, as a little girl, she had wanted to have her lobes pierced. "Are you having me on? I don't believe you!"

"If you want me to demonstrate," he said, "you will have to lie down."

They got up, and debated whether or not to fix the blackout, and agreed on keeping the dusk. They lay down on top of the bed side by side and he nibbled the lobe of her nearer ear; turning the key to open her cunt, he had called it. It made her giggle at first, then she went so still that he stopped to ask her if she were all right. "Go on, go on!" she pleaded: it was the nicest thing he had ever done to her. When he stopped again, she asked, "Now shall I do it to you?" He found her hand and laid it on his penis, which had shot up like a giant asparagus; she had not known that he had unbuttoned his trousers. "That's what it feels like," he said with much satisfaction.

She thought that it would crown the moment if she could get him to tell her what Chaim Weizmann had said. She asked him, and his penis wilted with the speed of air escaping from a balloon; he laid his hand over hers to make it remain where it was. He said, "I said that, when so many people are getting killed, it is a little thing to try to save one's parents, and he told me, 'He who saves one life saves as it were the world'. It's a quotation from the Talmud." Into the dark in which they could no longer see each other, he added, "Not that I mean to do no more than that."

SIX

AUGUST–SEPTEMBER 1941

(Sebastian)

WHEN SHE SENT Hamish her new address, she said something she could not afterwards remember that prompted him to write, "Did Hansi not tell you that I am a conscientious objector? I am sorry—" He could not manage a single letter, she had noticed, without being apologetic about something or other; she sometimes thought that he managed a babies' home because that was all he was good for. (As someone who frequently called herself a Jewish shit, she naturally did not think much of the people closest to her: could not see them as they were because they had not turned their backs on her.) This time he was sorry that she had apparently been misled.

She still knew almost nothing about him and felt that she could not, after exchanging letters, once a fortnight or so, for eight months, ask such basic questions as whether or not he was married, which she had not bothered with in the beginning because, mistaking him for his father, she had believed that she knew the answers; she was not going to ask Hansi after that doggerel she had sent her about him.

The bastard! Inge thought; it amused her to think it because he was, literally, a bastard—was he sorry that his father had abandoned him in some shieling instead of letting him grow up a Hitler Youth, would he have fought on the other side? But she could not bring herself to put an end to the correspondence, largely because—unlike Rudi—Hamish, who had never seen her, having only her writing to go on treated her as an adult.

"I don't know how Germany—how the world—can rid itself of Hitler without fighting," he answered her attack on his pacifism. "I don't claim to be able to solve anyone's problems, I just try to live with my own." She was willing to bet that they did not amount to much. On his mother's death he had sold their farm to finance his studies, which he had chucked at the beginning of the war as "irrelevant to the times"—he had been studying philosophy. Wanting to do his bit—"something more positive than killing"—he had started his home for orphaned and unwanted babies; he was sorry that he was good only for doing the paper work. I was right about him, Inge thought when she read this, and in respect of him lost her usual diffidence. He sent her a photograph of his staff and charges grouped on the lawn in front of the home; he was the one who was holding the oldest baby—whose hair was obscuring his face. She thought that it did not matter that she did not know what he looked like; she thought of Scotland as very remote and that they were unlikely to meet before she went on to Palestine, if that was where she was still going once this interminable-seeming war was over.

Wanting to hurt him without knowing why—perhaps because she could not, emotionally, afford to want to hurt Hansi (who she would have liked to have been and not only because Dolph loved her), and accepting that all Scotsmen were skinflints though she objected strongly to racial jokes about Jews, and unaware that she was betraying that pennies mattered to her—she wrote, "You don't have to send me stamped addressed envelopes to return your MSS, I can afford the postage." She re-used his envelopes—an acceptable wartime economy; when she found herself trying to think of a way of discouraging him from sending her things, she suspected herself of grudging the postage when the truth was that he was invading her with his writing. When she received a story which he had set in pre-war Germany and told in the first person through someone called Mendel, she felt almost detonated: the cheek of that bastard bastard, who would not fight the fatherland *über alles*! It was some days before she could make herself take another look, with the intention of slating the piece—and read it weeping until her tears smudged his ink. That he wrote better than she did she had accepted long ago and she was not troubled by it: did not disparage her talent as she did her self and knew that, anyway, writing was not a matter of competition; but she was upset by more than the story itself: she felt that she wanted to be, ought to be the one who had written it.

Mendel was still in her mind, in her dreams, perhaps, a few

nights later, when she was woken by the call of, "Jill, I want you! Inge, I need you!" or perhaps it was, "Jill, I need you! Inge, I want you!" or perhaps Sebastian's voice rang the changes. She jumped out of bed and groped her way to the window and in her haste to get it open tore the blackout; it was pitch-dark outside. "Jill . . . Inge . . ." the beloved voice roamed like a searchlight; either he was not sure of her window, though he had visited them while Dolph was there, or, more likely, he was drunk. Other people were opening their windows and demanding silence; there was the sound of something crashing into the street. Inge tried to call out but could not make herself do it: it was too embarrassingly public. She pulled her coat on—she still had no dressing-gown—and, snail-witted as she was even by daylight, realized that it would be quicker in the long run if she put her shoes on and if she laced them up; but she nearly locked herself out. By the time she reached the street he was no longer—if he ever had been—there; from a distance, from somewhere in the park, came the sound of revelry; she liked to believe that she would have endeavoured to find him if she had not had this reason for suspecting that he was not alone.

She was half-willing to believe that she had only dreamed or imagined it, but the next evening, when she got in from work, there was a letter for her, delivered by hand: he had been back—oh, Sebastian!—and she had not been there! "A thousand apologies," he wrote, he hoped that he had not compromised her with her neighbours. Worlds apart, she thought when she read this: what neighbour looking at her would believe that it was she who had been serenaded like that? He had been celebrating being taken off combat missions, and had wanted to say good-bye to her because he was being posted. "Far but not too far away," he wrote, and promised that there would be no repetition: he had made all his friends swear an oath to keep him away from her part of the town when he came to Leeds, as he would: she was his enchanted castle—and another thing was the friendship he felt for her brother.

She sat down at once in one of her writing rages, and wrote and tore up and started again and again, wasting half a packet of the expensive grey deckle-edged linen paper she used only for writing to him; all she said or tried to say has long been forgotten except this: she told him that she was not an English rose but a Jewish weed: trample on her and she would spring up again.

That letter was never finished or at least not sent; she mulled it over, re-reading his note until she reached the conclusion that what he had really meant but been too gentlemanly to say in so many words was that he had a thousand times over not meant it, had merely been drunk; all he had really said was, only a foreigner could have occasioned in me such un-English behaviour, better to have nothing more to do with you but your brother is different. And he had delivered his letter while she was out not because he had had to leave town but so as not to encounter her.

Eventually, it brought him an over-polite little missive such as one of Jane Austen's young ladies might have sent to the vicar.

She was more perverse in love than Rudi.

Dolph had left his birthday card for her with Sebastian who also sent one of his own, altering the words to read, *Many Happier Returns*; he had got a bookshop to post to her a copy of Daphne du Maurier's *Rebecca*. The book meant a lot to her not only because it came from Sebastian: she identified with the girl whose worth remained hidden from everybody including herself until discovered by the man who loved her.

When the manageress of the dress department heard that it was Jill's sixteenth birthday, she sent her out, as a treat, with pencil and paper, to make a note of what their competitors had in their window displays. What a use to put pencil and paper to, she was thinking, when there stood Mrs Duchamp, among the shoppers in the mid-morning sunshine, exclaiming, "Don't you recognize me, you funny girl!" She looked Inge over, her face creased with concern, until Inge looked down at herself thinking that there must be something wrong with her. "Your brother ..." Mrs Duchamp eventually suggested, and turned her head away with tears in her eyes. Wondering that she had ever disliked the woman, Inge explained why she was in black.

Mrs Duchamp instantly brightened up and began to draw her along. "Come and have a cup of coffee with me." Inge thought that perhaps it was an omen: but if this was the year in which her dreams would come true she did not want the first of them to be the one of sitting among the WVS women as if she were their equal. She managed to say that she did not have time as if she were sorry.

Mrs Duchamp still detained her, with a warm hand on her arm. "You must let us have your brother's address, we've been wanting to make up a little parcel for him—he so enjoys his food that it is a pleasure to feed him." Inge thought that perhaps middle-aged women preferred youngsters who could be cavaliers, to adolescent girls who showed up their age. "He's such a darling," Mrs Duchamp was saying. "Sebastian and he have become such friends. Only the other day, Sebastian told us that there was nothing he would not do for your brother!"

It was Mrs Duchamp's curse upon Inge; it was unintentional and Inge did not yet know it.

Rudi seemed to have forgotten her birthday.

She was thinking of Rudi fading out of her life, one morning, a Tuesday, towards the end of September, while she was ironing some dresses—she had dropped the iron and it was not working properly—when the department telephone rang. Somebody announced, "Jill Stone, to the office!" It was so reminiscent of Dovercourt that she could almost smell the murderous North Sea.

Going up in the staff lift she imagined being told that she should have been getting more money in her pay packet for the past month, ever since her sixteenth birthday; she would now get it in a lump sum and she wondered how much it would be; doing sums in her head she entered Personnel and was sent along to the general manager who stood up and shook her by the hand, gravely, as if she had saved the store from theft or fire. There was also a girl in airforce blue, who stubbed out her cigarette before standing up to greet her. Later in life Inge was unable to recall her exact words; she believed that she had said, "Sebastian—" but it must have been "Squadron-leader Duchamp"—"told me to bring you to the hospital." It conjured up Sebastian standing giving the order, and left Inge baffled.

Since Dolph had left for Lisbon, and Switzerland, and home, she had been more careful about going to the cinema; but she had already seen too many—had relished—films set in wartime Europe or pre-war Germany in which Jews and other opponents of the Third Reich were hunted and caught and tortured and occasionally killed but more often managed to escape, and now she believed that Dolph was one of them. The secret ways by which allied airmen shot down over Germany were got back to England had been used to rescue him, like Bobby Roberts, unhurt and gloating, raring to have another bash at the Boche—or perhaps not quite unhurt since Sebastian had sent his driver to take her to the hospital.

She must have gone back to the dress department for her handbag and gas-mask. Her navy blue school coat—still the only coat she had—had to be left every morning, after she had clocked in, in the staff cloakroom; it was on her arm when the WAAF girl opened the rear door for her before settling behind the wheel and driving off with such panache that Inge thought that she herself would never be able to join any of the women's services, when she had reached the age, because she was not good enough for them.

It was Dolph who had taught her—as he had taught her everything which, Jewish rubbish that she was, she had managed to learn—that there was only one right moment to every question; sitting forward on the edge of the seat she waited until they had left the town centre and she judged it time to ask, "Why?"—"Why what, dear?" the driver asked, kindly, and glanced at her over her shoulder. "Sit back and take it easy, my dear, I'll get you there as quickly as anyone can." Of course, Inge thought, Sebastian's driver would be the best on the base. Perhaps she had sounded not kind but patronizing—the thought made autumn leaves of all that was green in Inge. She did not know whether the right thing to do was to talk, or not to talk; it showed in her face, how ill-at-ease she was. "Are you all right?" the driver asked in a way which made Inge feel that she ought not to be—and then she remembered that Dolph was in hospital.

She was convinced that she was not upset: was merely holding herself in abeyance until the reunion, which she thought of as being happy; Sebastian's presence would be its grace note. When the driver suggested a cup of tea—she would get it for her in a jiffy—she did not want to stop, not because she thought of Dolph as dying but because she herself, as you say in English, was dying to see him. Eventually, the driver stopped anyway. Because of its association with Dovercourt, even the thought of the cup of tea she was to be given made her feel sick and she asked, very politely as if she might have been refused, for something fizzy—and got that red Tizer which was one day to be considered such a treat by her children.

They had been driving for a couple of hours or so before it occurred to her that she ought to have got police permission first; Dolph might move about England keeping no laws except his own: Dolph belonged among the people in high places—like Hansi. With a small haemorrhage of emotion she remembered Hansi; Rudi would have called it a Freudian forgetting. Just then the driver, making one more conscientious, final attempt to prepare the little fool for what was awaiting her, asked, "How long have you two known each other?" Inge realized that this was not a question anybody would ask her about her brother; but her mind, brimming with Dolph, would not admit the thought: she could not afford, just then, to let herself be confused.

At the hospital, she began to wonder if she were being mistaken for someone else: everybody was being so extraordinarily nice to her. They made her sit down out of the way and brought her one of their blessed cups of tea and stood about her, in their white coats, as if she were a freak. "Is this the girl?" they asked each other, and shook their heads because she looked so young. Then they stood aside to make way for Mrs Duchamp.

Even then, she did not begin to fear for Sebastian: he had written to her, not long before, that instructing tyros was a piece of cake; of course it would be that to him: he was as good with people as his father. She thought that Mrs Duchamp's presence there was a coincidence; with the assurance born of the need to continue to make sense of her misconception she thought, how nice of her to come and visit Dolph. Her WVS uniform looked as if it had been slept in, her hair had been tidied without the help of a mirror and her hand had been shaking when she made up her face. Taking all this in, Inge thought, wildly, George Eliot loved and even married somebody a lot younger than herself—while Mrs Duchamp took her funny little foreign former housemaid into her motherly arms.

The Doctor was also there and Inge thought that that was an explanation: Sebastian had summoned his father to look after Dolph and Mrs Duchamp had come along for the ride. The Doctor looked as if he had been slaving over a kitchen stove: red-faced and raw-eyed; he, too, took her into his arms but more as if he could not bear to look at her. He told her that she could go in, but only for a moment, and that she must not touch him: as well as internal injuries he had broken bones. She thought that Dolph must after all have been learning to parachute; there had been a time when he had talked of doing that. Perhaps the Doctor thought her stupid with shock; he repeated, "He has some broken bones and severe internal injuries," holding her back after opening the door for her, past it she could see the bedside table and on it her photograph; then—forgetting the one she had had taken according to his instructions for their parents—she knew for certain that it was Dolph because she had sent it to him while he was on the Isle of Man. Someone had propped it up for Sebastian in the hope that the sight of it would do him good. When she took a step forward and saw that it was he who was lying there she thought, Oh Mutti, I'm not me!

It had not occurred to her to fear for Sebastian because it would have meant believing that he would want to have her at his bedside.

No one had mentioned that there had been a fire when he had crash-landed the plane. The tyro co-pilot had been fried alive, she later overheard someone saying with English wartime humour. Sebastian's hair and eyebrows had been burned away, leaving him looking clownishly astounded; the right side of his face had scraped along the tarmac and looked as if it had not been cleaned. His wildflower blue eyes were cloudy with pain—drugs, too, but she did not think of that. "Good, you've come," he said as if she were all he needed. She was not even crying she was so happy.

Rudi was to say to her, "Anybody would have felt inadequate."

What she felt as she stood over him not knowing how to behave, was sorry that of all the girls in England he should have chosen her who had nothing to give him except utterly useless love. She said, "Darling, oh my darling!" an English word she had never yet used except to Georgie, and recalled that when a scout troop had come to Dovercourt to entertain them they had sung, *Oh my darling Clementine*, and was ashamed of herself, a would-be poet, for not finding at such a moment more original words. She put all she could of herself into her eyes, feeling, for the first time in her life, in every cell of her body, the honey of sexual passion. "Your father said that I mustn't touch you," she said. He blinked, slowly, acquiescing, and she said, "It doesn't matter," meaning that it did not matter to her though it did, agonizingly, unable to grasp that it might also matter to him. "I just want you to know that I want to." His left hand was undamaged; he offered it to her.

She knelt down so that she could take it without perhaps hurting his shoulder—not with the thought of getting closer to him; her one consolation afterwards was that, schooled by her brother, she had all along considered him more than herself. But the dead-coldness of his hand was unexpected and made her crave warm embraces; her tears were the sweat of frustration. He said, "Don't cry," and she stopped at once: that much at least she could do for him. She wanted to kiss his palm, because Dolph had told her that this signified devotion; she had to lay the hand down on the bed, not daring to twist the arm, before she could do it. What she felt then was sorry that he should love her, because it was swamping her love for him with gratitude. She felt that she was cheating him: because a Jewish refugee could not love as well as a non-Jewish Englishman.

"Get it done," he said, and she found that he was speaking over her head to his father, who laid a hand on her shoulder indicating that she should get up. She allowed herself to be led away, away from Sebastian, down the corridor and the steps and out of the hospital to a waiting chauffeur-driven car; she did not want to be troublesome to the Doctor and got into it because he expected it of her; they had passed through the hospital gates before she ventured to ask him, "Where are we going?" He drew her hand into his lap and patted it, and said, "We've got to go to Court, since we can't get hold of your parents and you're still a minor." She did not want to pester

147

him, and thought about it for a while before deciding that even Dolph would not have been able to work this out for himself, and asked, "What for?"

The Doctor gave her one of his swift appraising looks; perhaps he believed that he had already told her. "Permission for you to marry, girl," he said, a little impatiently.

At any other time she would have believed that he was joking. She would have liked to ask him, whom am I to marry? Her father would never have taken it upon himself . . . He was saying, "You do understand, don't you, that he is going to die? Nobody can live with his injuries, it would not be kind to try to prolong his life. Two-three days. Perhaps not even that." For a year and three weeks, she had loved Sebastian and expected his death, without preparing herself for it, without even realizing that she was unprepared. She thought that the Doctor, in his kindness, had found her a husband as a sort of compensation; she asked him after all, "Whom am I going to marry?" and found herself trembling violently and in his arms, believing that at last she understood: what Sebastian had been afraid of when he had called himself a coward had been this, his death; and now that it had come he wanted to give the people he most loved to each other in place of himself; she thought, I shall be their daughter-in-law and they'll be my family . . . . Round her neck was the green scarf put there by Mrs Duchamp because she had not wanted her to look as if she were in mourning, as if she were already in mourning.

On the steps of the town hall they were received by a policeman as if they had been expected. He led them down an echoing corridor lined with benches, on which hushed people, mainly children, were sitting, to a door which looked like all the others before which he said, "It won't take long, sir," to the Doctor as if they were there for his sake. But Inge thought that it took too long, for the bride of a dying man.

Perhaps he had meant that it would not take long once they were inside. The room was full of men, or they may have seemed many because one did not in those days see a lot of men together not wearing uniform. She was handed a Bible with a cross embossed on the cover; when they took it from her in exchange for another, slighter one, she thought, they won't let a Jew swear

148

on the New Testament—as if making this distinction amounted to discrimination against her. The man who questioned her, like a schoolmaster from above, wore neither wig nor gown; he must have been a magistrate but she thought of him as a judge: he was sitting in judgement on her.

When the facts had been got straight, he asked her, "Is there any pressing need for you to get married?" Inge looked round at the Doctor, who ought to have been the one to explain—had explained already—that Sebastian was dying; her imagination had rejected the thought and she was beginning no longer to believe it: there was no pressing need: they had the whole of their lives—wildly she thought of marriage as knotting lives together, so that if one contributed a longer piece than the other they could be adjusted, like ribbons, until they both had the same. "He means, are you pregnant?" the Doctor whispered to her. "No, no!" Inge said, remembering lying on the bed with Dolph. "Oh, no, we didn't!"

"Do you love him?"

For a moment she was not sure whether she was being asked about Dolph or about Sebastian. "Are you," the man asked with distaste, perhaps for her suspected lack of command of English, "as it is commonly put, in love with him?"

"No," Inge said, meaning that she did not wish to put it like that and by the man's reaction perceived her mistake. "I mean yes, I love him, I do love him, oh, I do!"

"Calm yourself," the man said, with a glance at the Doctor. She could not afterwards remember what else was said, before the man began a sort of summing up. "You were a servant in his parents' house, you knew, whenever he came on leave, that it might be for the last time: the chances were, you say, that he would get killed, but, you say, you did not let him into your bed—and yet you claim that you, eh—" as if she had no right to loving Sebastian, he finished—"are in love with him?"

Over her shoulder, the Doctor said, "She was under age, sir, she is only just sixteen." Inge believed that he was speaking on behalf of Sebastian: that he knew that if she had been sixteen then Sebastian would have wanted to come into her bed—he had shown no sign of it. Oh, Sebastian, she thought, in her new maturity, I would have welcomed you at any age!

"And now," the man said, making a show of patience with his hands, "you wish to marry him even though . . ." He looked at the Doctor and said, "I don't wish to distress the father . . . You have been told what his injuries amount to?" She wondered whether she had missed something the Doctor had said in Court: that Sebastian would never be able to beget that baby lying naked on a bearskin; in her confusion she thought that that explained the earlier question put to her about being pregnant. "What will you get out of it?" the man prompted her; it would have made more sense, she thought, if he had asked, what will Sebastian get out of it? "I shall survive," she answered, meaning that she would have the rest of her life to be, to have been his wife.

"Precisely," the man said, and leant back, with an air of finality and satisfaction. He leant forward again to say, "You came to this country as a refugee from Nazi oppression—" he read the phrase from her Alien's Registration Book and then looked at her over his glasses—"on condition that you would not stay for more than two years. That was nearly three years ago." Inge started to explain that because of the war . . . The man ignored this and continued, "As the wife—" he cleared his throat—"the widow of an airforce officer, not only will you be able to remain in this country but you will also be entitled to draw a state pension. To an English mind," he said, leaning forward as if he meant to spit on her, "this doesn't look like fair dealing!"

What upset her most was the thought of failing Sebastian: going back to the car she believed that what had been tested and found wanting was her love for him. After they had got in, as the car moved off, the Doctor said, "I am sorry to have exposed you to this, my dear."

She felt it as a seedcorn of coldness inside her that grew and spread until she was worse than dead: she was nothing. She asked, "Then Sebastian didn't . . . ?"—"Sebastian is in no condition to take thought for you or anyone, I knew he would have wanted it, he agreed at once, we promised your brother that we would look after you." Oh Dolph, Inge thought, this is the worst thing you have ever done to me.

She would never never never again love anyone, never again

expose herself to being made such a fool of! Who did she think she was that Sebastian—Sebastian!—loved her and wanted to marry her merely because she was Inge—she wasn't even Inge to him, to him she was Jill! That had not been love, that had been charity, Christian charity because she was to be pitied! What else was she good for except drowning like the girl in *The Bridge of Sighs*?

"My dear, he carried your photograph," the Doctor said.

But she could think, easily, of a dozen different ways in which he might have come by it, and none of them proved that he loved her; he must have been merely looking after it for Dolph: in Dovercourt, Rudi had always had something or other belonging to Dolph in his pockets. Thinking of Dovercourt, remembering how cagey the older girls had been about having themselves adopted, she said, "That's certainly one way of getting a housemaid for ever!"

"That isn't like you, Inge," the Doctor said, grieved for her, grieving over her, and she was instantly mollified because he had called her—for the first time—by her real name. But he could not now tell her, as he had meant to do to reconcile her to his wife, that it was she who had had the thought of sending for her when they had seen the photograph; the favour he had tried to do her had been an afterthought.

"I can't go back to the hospital!" Inge wailed, seeing that they were about to arrive there; she was hopelessly ashamed: confronted with that bogey from her childhood, that people would laugh at her; no wonder they had looked at her like that: having been told that Sebastian's—Sebastian's!—fiancée was coming, they had no doubt expected someone at least like Hansi: they must have felt properly swindled that it was only she.

But she had to get out of the car, and had not time to take off Mrs Duchamp's green scarf before the woman held her again in her arms and was telling her, "Just the same, you shall help me look after him!" She could hear that it was a genuine concession, not a trick to make her empty bedpans and clean up vomit which she would have been happy to do in any case. She thought, if I love him with all of me then perhaps even my love is enough?

But she felt that she could not face him. She had too much to tell him and could not say any of it, and not only because his body had been so injured. To have mistaken his kindness for love meant having taken advantage of his helpless state to get from him more than he had meant to give her. But she felt also angry with him because if he had not been as he was she would not have been so misled.

Rudi was to ask her if Sebastian had known that he was dying: because if he had agreed to marry her, expecting to live, was that not proof that he loved her? She did not think of that at the time: when his father came out to where she was funking it in the corridor, and urged her to come along, Sebastian was waiting, and she went with him and saw that, meanwhile, they had rigged up a blood-transfusion, it did not occur to her that it might have been done to give him hope; it gave hope to her.

The transfusion went into his left wrist so that he could no longer move even that freely; he summoned her with his eyes and she trotted to what, in spite of herself, she thought of as her place beside him. As she knelt down he said, "Sorry," and she found in herself, unexpectedly, a scrap of her brother's self-control, massive when it was needed, and said, "It doesn't matter;" one born to England could not have done it better.

She said, "I won't hold you to it. I mean if—" for once she hoped to be able to trade on her foreign origin as she corrected herself—"when, I mean when you get better, I won't—" with a little toss of her head she achieved a joke—"sue you for breach of promise." The good side of his mouth twitched: to smile? to speak? He gave up the effort and she blundered on, "Tell you what, let's forget about it. If you really meant it you will have to ask me again." But she did not believe that he would, not even if he lived to be a hundred and twenty.

His eyes were like wildflowers carried for too long in a child's fist and past reviving in water. She thought, I don't care if he doesn't love me; and prayed, Oh God help me to be of some use to him; but it was her mother remembered who came to her aid. "Think of that blood going into you as a regiment of soldiers," she began, as her mother had used to talk her to sleep. "No, let's make that a peaceful image, think of bricks: think of the bricks lining up to make a row, with another row on top and another to make a wall, they're making you as strong as a wall,

Sebastian, as strong as a house ..." His eyelids, one black-skinned, one skinless, were closing and perhaps he was already past hearing, unconscious or asleep, when she said, "... as strong as a home, Sebastian, you are my home." Only then did her fingers thieve the touch of his left hand.

Later she thought that what had been most hurtful about that marriage business had been that it had put her at the receiving end: as if as a Jewish refugee she had nothing to give—when all she wanted was to be generous to Sebastian. She could almost love even Mrs Duchamp, for entrusting him to her to the extent of leaving her alone with him, though it was not for long: she and the Doctor came and sat down next to each other on chairs placed on the other side of the bed; Mrs Duchamp wept and whispered; the Doctor occasionally grunted, involuntarily like a man asleep; when she was rash enough to meet the eyes of either they smiled at her.

In the almost three years she had been in England she had not, altogether, been smiled at as much, or so it seemed to her then, as during those hours when his parents and the doctors and nurses who came and went believed that Sebastian loved her. She almost suspected herself of having lulled him to sleep so that he would not betray her; but it is the truth that she would not have cared what he said, if he had had strength enough to speak she would have rejoiced at it.

Towards evening, when the effect of the morphine he had been given wore off, and the next injection was being delayed so that it would see him through the night, it seemed to his mother and to Inge that he was beginning to recover. With his valiant patience, he listened to his mother's plans for him, and then turned his bruised eyes to Inge. "Tell me a story," he pleaded, precisely as Dolph had used to do when anything ailed him. "About when you were little," he prompted; he did not need to take thought: just by being Sebastian he made things better for all about him. She thought then that her life was like a ring, with him as its diamond: he was the reason why it was there but of course there had to be more to it than that.

When it was time for them to leave him, his mother came round the bed to kiss the good side of his face. The Doctor had to turn Inge back from the door: she did not want to presume;

but she also did not want Sebastian to doubt that she could love his ruined body. She took her time over kissing him, more time than his mother had done who had kissed him often, and afterwards, directed by his eyes, put her hand where he could lay his fingers about it which was the only response he could make.

"You'll have bucked up by tomorrow morning!" were the last jolly English words she said to him.

His parents were being accommodated within the hospital; only when leaving it, with one of Sebastian's nurses going off duty, did Inge remember that she ought to have got permission from the police. She decided not to bother: the worst they could do to her, she thought, was to imprison her on the Isle of Man and if Sebastian died she would not care and if he lived then she would care even less; she was not going to make another request to the English authorities and run the risk of being refused again.

They were not keen to allow her into the hotel—it was full of the relations of the men who were in the military hospital—because her people were at war with them; it was rather tactless of her to show up there, the manageress told the nurse, and Inge thought, blasphemously, if I had been carrying Sebastian's bastard, which would have made the judge approve of me, then would there have been room for me in the inn? Perhaps they really were overcrowded; she was given one of the servants' rooms though they put clean sheets on the bed.

She had been told, would she please take her breakfast early; she did not bother with it but stole out of the hotel—the nurse had already signed for the bill—and in the dawn drizzle returned to the hospital. She had grown worried in the night that Sebastian, if he had been aware that she had doubts, might have misunderstood them: she had decided that for the time being she would pretend to believe that he loved her. Having half convinced herself, the better to be able to persuade him, she walked up the steps and through the swing doors with an assurance which really amounted to no more than knowing the way, but because the surroundings were unfamiliar it made her feel that she was capable of coping with anything. That none of the staff seemed to recognize her did not alarm her: they all looked alike to her in their hospital uniforms and she felt that she was making a fool of herself by saying good-morning to strangers. They were all in a hurry and she prayed, Please God don't let Sebastian be the emergency, and amended that hastily, guiltily, to, Please God don't let there be one! Dolph would have felt like disowning her: he had told her more than once that if he were God he would piss on her if she only remembered him whenever she wanted something. Please God just this once, she prayed—and saw that the recess outside Sebastian's door, where they had waited the day before, was empty. Are they not yet up or have they gone in? she wondered, as if there could be no other explanation.

When she saw that the door for which she had been making stood open, showing that the room was unoccupied, the bed stripped, what she thought was that she must have made a mistake. She looked round for someone to ask and saw what nurses there were further along the corridor vanishing into the walls. She had turned back, to find her way better by starting again from the entrance, when some white-coated man came up behind her, laid a fatherly hand on her shoulder and said, "I am sorry, we did all we could."

She could not take it in. When somebody said, "Would you like to see him?" and led the way, she followed believing that he had been moved to another part of the hospital, where other doctors would be able to do more for him. They must have thought it strange—un-English—of her to hurry along to the mortuary as if it were a good place to get to.

It was full of green pot-plants and colourful bunches of flowers, with several biers; she saw other dead faces—the nurse who was with her, in searching, uncovered them although surely there must have been labels?—and then she saw Sebastian's. She looked at it asking herself: about him, that stranger, I have had all those emotions? The right side had been cleaned and rounded out with something pretending to be flesh; it had been done lovingly by someone who most probably had not known him in life and who had been up all night; it was the thought of what people did for one another that moved her, more than grief. Wanting to stay but have something else to look at, she turned to the altar; it came to her as the shape of an aeroplane before she saw the cross; beneath it candles were burning and they must have reminded her of some Jewish ceremony out of her childhood because the sight of them made her feel guilty: as if her being in that alien place could still harm her forebears confronting the Inquisition.

SEVEN

OCTOBER 1941–FEBRUARY 1942

(Rudi)

HAMISH WROTE, "SHALL we follow the majority and say that words are useless or shall we say, with Yeats, 'Words alone are certain good'? You must milk your grief, Inge!" She had already begun doing that, but found his way of putting it distasteful: betraying, she thought snobbishly, his peasant origin. The letter continued about Fiona, who had been dumped, new-born, in a dustbin and was his latest pet, with him the clock round so that, even at night, when she cried he could hold her, "feeling useless but loving". Maybe she would rather have stayed in her dustbin, Inge thought, I would in her place, who is he to play God? In the midst of his account, as if he were talking and could not stop himself, he interrupted himself with "Oh, Inge, I am so sorry . . ." Inge screamed into the silence of her bed-sitter, wordlessly, until her landlady knocked on the door to ask if she were all right.

The letter finished soon after, as if he had run out of things to say though he rarely did, and she was surprised to get another the next day only because she had not expected him to be so lavish with his stamps. "I am sorry that I did not think of it at once—" he had done but hesitated—if there were nothing now to keep her in Leeds, would she not join him, for a visit or indefinitely, as his guest or as a helper . . . ? "I would so very much like to be of some use to you." The cheek of that bastard! Inge thought. Begotten by the enemy on a Scottish whore . . . . She had no idea why she was so angry with him but it did her good to curse another instead of herself. In the night, weeping in her sleep and waking herself up with it, she at once started raging against him, who does he think he is, useless bastard, useless even to his babies: he said so himself. Who does he think he is that I should need him, when I can do without Sebastian, without Dolph, without Mutti and Papa, without Georgie, without Mother and Dad, without Jesus, without Germany, without the Promised Land ... the list could be extended endlessly.

She would have liked to write and tell him, I don't need you; and certainly, with Dolph's things in the attic to make her feel at home, she no longer needed him as her keeper of manuscripts. But she had to have someone with whom to share her addiction to words. She was some distance yet from submitting her work to editors but after Sebastian's death she bought her first typewriter, second-hand, hard to come by and expensive in wartime; she bought it before she owned a wristwatch or a winter coat; Rudi commented that with it—a step towards getting published—she was trying to make the world take the place of Sebastian.

It wasn't a bad time for Rudi. The captain who had been hounding him was replaced by Captain Thomas, who was aware that the labour battalion consisted largely of intelligentsia. He discovered that Rudi was able to give him a good game of chess, and could hold his own in any conversation— and that he was nearing the end of his tether. He got him a job in the company office and befriended him in various smaller ways. He was a young man—though not as young as Rudi, who was then twenty—studious, shy, rather enigmatic; he had been wounded at Dunkirk and had the Military Cross—the whole mix was designed to make Rudi believe himself madly in love. Unfortunately for him, the Captain was happily married; to begin with he had even discounted what was rumoured about Rudi—so much for Dolph's self-reproaches in Dovercourt. When he learned that Rudi meant to spend his next leave in the nearest town, in the hope of seeing him there, he packed him off to stay with his wife, evacuated to a two-centuries-old tin-miner's cottage on Bodmin Moor. It was paradise to Rudi who wrote from it to Jill, some time in July, that no doubt the Captain had instructed his wife to treat him like a prince: he was not even allowed to chop the kindling for the kitchen range.

Inge was jealous.

She wrote back reminding him that she had moved to Leeds

for his sake, and in the year she had been there had seen him once, briefly, between trains; there was Dolph's room and she too could put him up; what could Mrs Thomas offer him that she couldn't? and in addition she had running hot water. If he had outgrown his old friends, hobnobbing as he was with captains and their wives—though when she wrote this she still had her squadron-leader—she would cross his name out of her address book which was full enough even without it.

What was the joke? Mrs Thomas asked him when she saw his self-satisfied grin, and Rudi told her about Jill; to his shame it must be said that he did so as a way of singing for his supper. Mrs Thomas advised him—as who, knowing the facts, wouldn't have done?—to let it ride. He did not even send Jill a card on her birthday.

After Sebastian's death, when she was travelling, alone, by train, back to Leeds, she felt the need to unburden herself to someone, and whom else did she have? She filled almost half a writing-pad with scribble scribble scribble—as another would have used up a pile of handkerchiefs weeping; instead of sending this—she was growing up—she wrote him a note, saying merely that she needed him, if he "could spare the time between sailors". Rudi liked her to make jokes and she was, in her bereaved state, trying to please him: to make him remember that she, too, could be good company; Rudi believed that she had found him out and was intrigued—always bird-lime to catch a Rudi.

He arrived one evening late in November, with the collar of his greatcoat turned up about his reddened ears, his reddened nose running. "I think I'm going to have a cold," were the first words he said to her after thirteen months, and even the sense of anticlimax brought her such a whiff of Dolph that she caught hold of him and drew him over the threshold and, standing on tiptoe, kissed his cold damp face—giving him all the welcome she had never given and now never would give to Sebastian.

She had the whole flat to herself; the people who had just moved out had left a bag of coal for her under the stairs and she had built up her fire to rival Mrs Thomas's; she had two weeks' meat ration simmering as goulash in the oven. It occurred to Rudi then that when he had caught sight of her and her brother struggling to get on to the boat-train, he had fallen in love with the pair of them, with their being siblings. He took her head between his hands, his cold thumbs on her cheekbones, his cold fingers deep in her hair, and kissed her eyes: the tenderest gesture which had ever been shown to him. It was the tenderest gesture which had ever been shown to Inge.

He had brought her a bunch of fox-red chrysanthemums; no one had ever before thought of giving her flowers. "Oh, Rudi!" she exclaimed, and did not know that she was going to tell him, "I've been wanting to kill myself."

He could not cope with such intensity. "And leave me to eat up all by myself whatever it is I can smell so deliciously cooking?" he asked, pushing past her. "Oh, Rudi!" she exclaimed again, but on a lighter note.

She took care of her bunch of flowers, and ran his bathwater, while he went up to make himself at home in David's attic; before he had finished undressing he could hear her singing. Her passion for babies arose out of her need to do small practical things for other people which she thought of as making use of her capabilities. "Mrs Thomas gave me a whisky in my bath!" he called from beyond the bathroom door and again she burst out with her, "Oh, Rudi!" this time stricken because she had not thought of buying whisky for him. He had his work cut out persuading her that he had only been joking.

David's trousers were too baggy in the seat and too short in the legs for him, but a white cable-stitch roll-neck sweater set off his curly black hair and his fine dark eyes. Satisfied with what he had got from the mirror, he went down the stairs wishing that his Captain could see him—until he saw himself reflected in Jill's eyes. "Oh, it's nice to have you here, Rudi," she said warmly: seeing him in civvies had taken her right back to the time when she had loved him.

"I feel almost human," he said; she thought that it was only his way of talking; preceding him into the kitchen she made some comment about it being still better if he could have worn his own clothes. "But I haven't been able to do that for more than a year now," he told her rashly, and she looked at him over her shoulder as she dished out their food, to see if he could mean that they no longer fitted him; she knew that his relations had not been bombed out: had moved for the duration to some-where in the home counties. "Why ever not?" she asked with more than half her mind on the food.

He was seduced by the warmth: the feeling of being at home, which was the fault of the kitchen and Jill's treating him as if he were her brother; it was making his heart discharge as well as his nose. He told her, "Because my dear relations have washed their dear hands of me." He clamped his mouth shut after the words, his lips a thin line, and looked at Jill as if she were booby-trapped.

"But why?" she asked.

"Because of the sailors," he said.

Dolph-David had forgotten to enlighten her on homosexual-ity.

Being Rudi, he realized his mistake at once and changed the subject, tried to be amusing about his beastly journey, com-plimented her on her inexpert cooking, and was appalled at what he had got himself into when she said, between mouthfuls—well-brought-up little girl that she was—"You'll have to explain that to me."

"They don't approve of me," he prevaricated.

She put her fork down and cast a look upon him as if she meant it as a protective cloak. "Oh, Rudi!" Rudi turned pink. He got up and made a show of hunting for his cigarettes, though he had them in his—or rather David's—pocket. "Is that why you stayed with Mrs Thomas?" she asked; what he found touching, more than that she was so transparent, was that she was unaware of it. "Because you weren't able to go home?"

"I haven't got a home," he said, sounding tetchy: he thought that this at least was a point which she ought to have got by now; she did not have his gift for empathy and believed that he was embarrassed because once upon a time she had thought him the cat's whiskers. His hands were shaking as he lit his cigarette, to give himself something to do, and at once put it out again because they had not finished eating. "Well?" he asked her, meaning, help me.

She thought that he meant, what do you think of that? as if he did not have her face opposite to tell him. She asked, "What did you do to upset them, Rudi?" He turned a shade pinker as his eyes shied away from hers. He said, "So you think it must be my fault? of course, everything always is. I might have known that you would be on their side."

"But I'm not, I'm not!" she exclaimed, jumped up and came round the table to kneel at his feet. "I think you're . . . you're . . . Next to Sebastian, and of course Dolph, you are the nicest person I've ever come across. I don't understand why they . . ." She looked at him meltingly, as if she were chocolate sauce and he a pudding. He put a hand out to tuck a strand of her hair behind her ear; it was a gesture out of her childhood and he had probably seen her brother making it, though he would certainly not have copied it consciously. "They've done more than throw me out," he told her. "They've blocked my bank account. It wouldn't matter so much if it weren't becoming possible even for enemy aliens to apply for a commission." He shut up and she, eyes shining, prompted him, "You're going to be an officer, Rudi?"—"How can I?" he asked as if it were her fault. "Being as poor as a church mouse."

She thought about it and then told him, "Dolph left me some money."

"And sharing my relations' poor opinion of me, you think that I'd take it?" She had been resting her hands on his knees, for balance; certainly, he thought, unaware of what she was doing—perhaps misled by her brother's trousers—she was moving her palms along his thighs. He stood up to shake them off, and found himself in a passion.

Even talking of his disgrace, he thought, was preferable to that.

She saw him looking at his watch—too early, he thought, to plead the hour in order to escape her—and said, "Why don't you go and sit by the fire while I do the washing-up, and then I'll make us some coffee." He looked not restored by the food, as Dolph had done in the airforce club, but as if the effort of eating it had been too much for him. But he would not consent, either to drink coffee so late in the evening or to let her treat him, as Mrs Thomas had done, like a prince. To divert her attention he asked after the Duchamps.

She had not seen them again. As soon as she had got back to Leeds she had written to them that it had all been a misunderstanding: she knew how Sebastian had come by her photograph: her brother had left it lying about that time when he had stayed with them and he had pocketed it to keep it safe for him—she wrote that she knew this for certain. She would have liked to have added, Sebastian told me so, but could not bring herself to lie about him, only about her Dolphin and herself. (She now called her brother that because it made him sound safe and harmless, and conjured him up less well then the first syllable alone. This was when she got into the habit of spelling his name with a ph so that even now to write Dolf, as it once was, looks wrong.) She had never loved Sebastian, she wrote, she did not expect them to forgive her for not speaking out in the hospital but she had felt too sorry for them all, "as only a Jew can feel sorry", she wrote for Mrs Duchamp's benefit. And of course, the judge had been right: it was precisely for the reasons he had mentioned in his summing up that she had wanted Sebastian to marry her. How could she have loved him? She had hardly known him! Was it not true that Sebastian himself had told them that he would do anything for her brother? It was for her brother's sake that he had agreed to the marriage.

The magistrate, she told Rudi as they finished the washing-up, had enquired about her parents and she had had to tell him that she was able to exchange letters with them through the Red Cross. He had also got out of her that she had not as much as mentioned Sebastian's name to them. "I couldn't explain to him, Rudi, you understand, don't you?" she asked, her tears—tears for Sebastian—flowing as from a broken water-pipe; they both ignored them. All she was able to write were twenty-five words including her signature. Before then, in the proper letters which she had been able to send them through Dolph while he was interned, she had tried to sustain them by claiming that she was engaged to Rudi. "I might as well be," she told him as they settled down in her room by her extravagant fire, with a nice cup of tea. "I shall never be able to marry an Englishman—I should always suspect myself of having done it for the reasons that man said."

"Well, you can't marry me either," Rudi said with his nose in his cup. She pretended not to have heard him.

After a while he told her, "My uncles, in the days when they cared what would become of me—" Inge thought this one of the saddest things she had ever heard anyone say—"tried to marry me off; there were always plenty of eligible girls about, for my eligible boy cousins. But as soon as any of them began to show an interest in me, one of my aunts would take the mother aside and the next thing I knew, the poor girl had been packed off to Canada, or worse." He sounded triumphant.

"Wouldn't you like to get married, Rudi?" Inge asked.

"I'd be a rich man if I did," he told her.

But he managed to change the subject and to relax—though not to the extent of stopping to chain-smoke—while they listened to music and between records planned their week: she, of course, would have to go to work. Relieved when he found that it was ten o'clock, he rashly said, "Time I were in my bed—" and remembered that it was David's; just then he would have given the rest of his life to have David in it, and not for his own sake. The thought of David, a solitary commando, in wartime Germany, kept him at his sister's fireside. Inge, misunderstanding his reluctance to leave her, said, "It's cold upstairs," and explained that she had thought of buying an electric fire but was afraid that it would make the new landlord unwilling to continue to include the electricity in the rent. Rudi, looking at her, thought, she ought to be worrying about a new party frock or her backhand at tennis . . . . She caught his look and said, "You don't have to go upstairs;" he thought that she meant, since the rest of the flat was empty. Growing rosy, she said, "If you like you can share my bed."

"My dear Jill," he said, standing up prior to going, "you make a charming hostess. But don't you think that that is carrying hospitality a bit far?"

"Oh, Rudi!" she chirruped and tried to get into his arms. He took hold of her by the shoulders to keep her away from him, while she explained that she needed deflowering, and that her brother had told her to get it done by someone who understood her. "I know that you like me, but I don't attract you, is that it?"

"No," he said, more to his irresponsible cock than in answer. The girl was not even offended; genuinely curious about the adult world she was so impatient to get into, she asked, "Your taste is more Mrs Thomas?"

164

"My taste is more Mrs Thomas's husband," he told her.

It was he who had given her her leather-bound copy of Oscar Wilde's complete works; he had hinted at the background to *The Ballad of Reading Gaol*—she had forgotten that. He could see her thoughts scuttling about behind her puckered forehead and closed his eyes against what she would say. What she said was, "Poor Rudi!"

That night he managed to parry her questions with the argument that if they talked any more then, neither of them would be able to sleep, and in the morning, when she brought him a cup of tea before trotting off to work, he pretended successfully to be asleep. In the course of the day he bought tickets for the Yiddish theatre, and for a variety show—Inge blamed herself for not finding this to her taste; on other evenings they went to the cinema. He met her after work and introduced her to that wartime institution, the British Restaurant, where good meals were to be had cheaply. When she had first been a foster-child, and Mrs Sparrow had asked her to choose a toothpaste, she had opted for Odol, known to her from home; at the beginning of the war this had reappeared in a new package marked, *British made for British teeth*; she had always felt that she was not entitled to fill her Jewish refugee stomach in a British Restaurant.

There came a day when she insisted that they must spend the evening at home so that they could talk. To delay their arrival, Rudi made them walk back, collecting fish and chips on the way; he must have been desperate: all that distance in his army boots! By the time they arrived his nerves were in such a state that he had to keep his hands in his pockets, which made things still worse for him because he could not smoke. In the course of the day, he had provided the flat with a fresh selection of records and with books to entertain her, but she would not be side-tracked and asked him—she had had time to choose her opener—"Are you differently made?"

He almost choked on a chip. When he could speak he exclaimed, "Certainly not!" and saw that she was hurt because he had snubbed her. "If you mean, was I born this way, the answer is also almost certainly not." It was as if she had pulled a stopper out: he began to relieve himself of his past uncontrollably, as if it were vomit; he kept trying to get away from the stench of it and she needed to follow him all over the flat, to keep with him.

He had been an only child, parked by his parents whenever they wished to be rid of him with an aunt who had two daughters of about his age. They were very fond of dressing up, one of his earliest memories was of dressing up, like them, as a witch or a fairy. But soon he thought too much of himself for this and began to improvise his own costumes. One day he dressed up as a slave, in no more than a loincloth, with a rope tied about his neck and with raspberry jam sores; that was his undoing. When his cousins took him along to show him off to their mother, she happened to have a couple of women friends with her, who entered into the spirit of the game, pretending that they wanted to buy him which gave them an excuse for fingering him all over—pinching him, scratching him with their rings, and tickling him, he could still recall the feel of it. "That night," Rudi said, "was the last peaceful night of my life—and it wasn't very peaceful." With much whispered joking which was, literally and metaphorically, above his head, they had promised to make him a present. "I lay awake trying to guess what it was I was to be given, a guitar perhaps—my cousins had guitars—or something really exciting like a pony—they had ponies, too; they had a lot of things which it did not occur to my parents to get for me." It took him a while, after mentioning his parents, still in Germany, to pick up the thread.

He was told to look for his present and found it, after much searching, rather predictably in the dressing-up-box: a devil's outfit which must have been got at a theatrical costumier's; it was wrapped round a sort of truncheon.

"What was it?" Inge prompted.

"That's what I asked," Rudi told her, by now pink to the peaks of his ears. "I was soon to find out." But it was a long time before he could make himself begin to disgorge again.

This time his aunt came to fetch him; he alone was to come with her—she sent her daughters off to play their guitars or to ride their ponies or something. She had the same two friends with her, and again they admired him and paid him compliments—what fine black curls, what fine dark eyes, what long sensitive fingers; then they showed him what, being the devil, he had to do with the dildo. It was a word Inge did not know but she thought it wiser not to interrupt him. They kept him at it for what seemed to the boy a long time; then they stripped him naked and, all three of them, raped him.

Into his silence Inge asked, "How old were you?" and when he told her, twelve, she tried to remember what her brother had been like at that age; she was not sure that she had understood him but did not think that she could very well ask him, how rape? Instead she asked, "Why didn't you scream for help or run away from them?"

His aunt had threatened him: she would write to his father that she had found him with his hand in her purse, and/or that the maids had complained that he was molesting them; he was not close to his father but he would have gone through fire if that had been necessary to keep his good opinion. But she had written to him, anyway, and in addition to her other satisfactions had had that of knowing that he had been beaten, twice: once for doing whatever he was supposed to have done and once for not owning up to it. His father, who prided himself on being a modern man, had got the chauffeur to do it. And the chauffeur had afterwards taken him up to his room and been nice to him. "Don't ask me what *he* did," Rudi said.

"I wasn't going to," Inge said, having heard as much as she could bear on his behalf, for the moment. After a while she asked, "Did you tell all this to Mrs Thomas?"

"Certainly not, Mrs Thomas is a lady!" It was the expression on his face, when his brain caught up with his mouth, that made Inge realize what he had as good as said. He was still trying to find words of apology when she told him, "It's all right! If being a lady means that you wouldn't have told me then I'm glad that I am not one." In their private language, being a lady became a term of abuse. "I haven't ever told anybody," Rudi said, and saw that he could not have paid her a greater compliment.

"Not even Dolph?" she asked, and he answered at once, "Especially not David!" with such vehemence that she suddenly understood him. After a while she asked, "And something of what you feel for my brother rubs off on me?"

He got up to go, saying that they both needed time to be

167

alone; but he remained standing by the open door; Dolph's trousers were not so baggy that they concealed what had happened to him. Inge stood up to go to him, but he came back and took her in his arms; they were to discover that his penis was cocky enough—until they tried to take advantage of it.

The new people moved in the next day; in her mind, Inge cursed them with all the swear-words she had learned from Sebastian; but it worked out to what she then thought was her advantage: Rudi thought twice about leaving her fireside when it meant perhaps meeting strangers on the way if he were to change his mind and come back.

It was enough for Inge just to have him in her bed; she felt that to have done more would have been rushing things. "We're a pair," she said, holding him in her arms. "You love Dolph and I love Sebastian and all we have is each other."

Later that night she asked him, "What did you mean when you said that if you got married you'd be a rich man?" He explained that the family had a trust fund for helping its young people to set up house. "Well, let's do that!" she exclaimed. "Let's set up house together!" The words themselves enchanted her.

In the morning, the last of his leave, she decided not to go to the store; they made the round of the post offices in search of international reply coupons: Red Cross letters were no good without them. They managed to get three, and used them all: the letters sometimes got delayed for months or lost. She could ask her parents to give their permission to marry *him*, she argued; she was not going to run the risk of having to go before another magistrate: some day his cock would become amenable and supposing she became pregnant? "Just in case," she said, and posted the three identical letters on the way to the station.

Hansi also, before the end of the year, spent one of her leaves in Leeds; she had not done so sooner, for one reason or another, chiefly in an attempt to bully Inge into meeting her at Hamish's in Scotland—which Inge refused to do, pleading that she could not afford it, when the truth was that, to her mind, there was something patronizing about Hansi's attempt at matchmaking.

But when Hansi wrote that she was coming to Leeds, Inge was

overjoyed, thinking that next best to having her brother back would be to have his girl with her. She saved up her ration coupons and planned their meals, and—with Rudi's example to follow—entertainments for their evenings together. She even washed the bedspread and the curtains in the attic because Rudi had smoked so much up there, in case Hansi objected to the smell. But she went to meet her at the station still undecided whether or not to give her her own bed to sleep in: if she had been Hansi, being able to undress beside a fire and getting into a more comfortable bed would not have mattered to her as much as lying down to dream among David's belongings.

She need not have worried. Hansi had not come to Leeds to stay with her, had not come on her own; when Inge's face betrayed her as she realized it, Hansi said, "There'll be all the time when you are at work—when you aren't I shall send my friends packing." As if she were not also a friend! They were another ATS girl and a lanky Free Pole. But the first time he cleared off and Inge tried to get rid of the other girl, that one said, "You can say anything you like in front of me, Hansi and I are like sisters."

"I've nothing to say," Inge told them both; herself she told, I never meant to tell her about Rudi, I never expected her to be waiting for me when I got in from work, with a meal ready, as if she were Mutti! She thought, fuck Hansi, that's all she is good for, she's certainly no good to me!

And fuck her the Free Pole probably did. Inge was growing up and could read the signs. She did not blame him: heads turned at the sight of Hansi, she was whistled after, accosted in the streets. She did not exactly blame Hansi, her knowledge of the Dolphin would not let her: he would say that by giving to another what he was not there to claim for himself she was not doing him out of anything; he would want her—wherever he was, oh Dolph, oh Dolphin!—to have a good time.

It was Hansi's attempt to deceive Inge that Inge could not forgive her: it smacked of patronage. Dolph might have called it useful conditioning for dealing with Rudi's relations, that for a week Inge felt obliged to be pleasant to people she did not want to be with, people whose company made her feel only the more alone.

*   *   *

Early in the new year she received two relevant letters. One was from "Aunt Ruchamah": her brother had on the strength of his false papers been conscripted into the Wehrmacht and had had to work his way back from the Russian front. He had arrived at his parents' home no more than days after they had been taken for resettlement in the east; having ascertained that the next transport from the town was destined for the same Latvian ghetto, he had sewn a yellow star on his coat, registered with the Jewish community, and persuaded some clerk to substitute his name for that of another young man.

Joachim Meyer, Inge thought when she read this; she did not know—few people then knew—what was meant by resettlement.

The other letter was from her parents, giving her and Rudi their blessing; it was the last Red Cross letter she was to receive from them.

Rudi wrote that, through the good offices of Captain Thomas, he managed to have a telephone conversation with Hector, the one of his cousins who had always been friendliest: his father was the uncle who had emigrated to the USA when war broke out and would have taken Rudi if the family had let him. Rudi had wanted Hector to sound out the family, especially his eldest uncle—who had been received in audience by Queen Victoria and was in his eighties—and was Rudi's official guardian. He did not know what Hector had told the family, Rudi wrote, but the result had been a flood of letters from his relations, the gist of which was that they wanted to know who she was. "I couldn't tell them that you're a shop-assistant," he wrote, "they wouldn't understand, or rather, they would totally misunderstand." In view of her age he had had to tell them that she was still at school. He had had to make up another lie about where she was staying, he explained, as they had demanded her address. "I wouldn't put it past them to descend upon you, and you wouldn't have liked that and neither would they." Captain Thomas sent his regards and was doing his best to get him a commission in the Intelligence Corps.

Would his relations not think her good enough for him? Inge wrote back, with mixed feelings: what sort of girl did they think would be willing to marry Rudi? They should think themselves lucky! Something of this must have come through in her letter: Rudi wrote back that she ought to forget about setting up house with him—reminding her that it had been her idea. Feeling lonely and full of doubts about himself, and, not least of all, cold lying alone between damp blankets under canvas, he had already broken the resolution he had made in her bed—and not told her about because he had known that he would break it. He was no good to her, he wrote, he was not even a decent human being: he had gone along with her idea of marriage only because he did not see how else he could afford to take a commission, and in the Pioneer Corps even as an NCO—he had now got his second stripe—he was going to the dogs . . . . The time was past when that phrase alone would have been enough to comfort Inge. She was wondering whether she could possibly write to Captain Thomas—she did not know quite what it was she wanted to ask him—when he wrote to her, less in his capacity as Rudi's superior officer, he explained, than as his friend: he understood that her own position was not easy but unless she was sure that she could cope without Rudi getting hurt it would be better if she were to break off their engagement.

In the three years since Dovercourt, she had turned to Rudi whenever she needed a second opinion—but who was going to give her advice about her adviser? True, in the past summer she had almost lost touch with him, but that was when she had still had Sebastian, and when the Dolphin was no further away than Spain, than Switzerland. She realized that if she rejected Rudi now she would have to give him up altogether: no more letters to and from him, and she could not face this in addition to all her other losses.

And so she wrote to him, "We have my parents' permission to get married."

His relations were clamouring to meet her, he wrote back; they were asking, when would she next be in London—they lacked the imagination to conceive of anyone within their sphere as living an existence which was different from their own. Perhaps it was partly his fault: he had told them, after all truthfully, that she had a little money. They wanted her to take tea with them in Brown's Hotel or in Harrods—the choice should be hers. Inge rightly assumed that they believed that it would tell them something about her though she had no idea what, and that they did not want to have her in one of their houses until they had looked her over; but she was deceiving herself when she believed that she would have accepted an invitation to stay with them. Rudi wrote that it would mean spending a night or two in London: it would also give her an opportunity to shop. The bombing just now was not so bad—which was true—and in any case she ought not to let this deter her: the Londoners didn't. She should not worry about using up the money David had left her, he would soon be able to replace it with as much as she could want.

How shall I live with all these lies? Inge wondered, and wrote back that she was most definitely not going to meet any of Rudi's relations without his being there, she would "feel too outnumbered". She told herself that if he did not understand that, then she would have nothing more to do with him. But being Rudi of course he understood, and not only agreed but suggested a way out: he had talked the problem over with Captain Thomas, who would be writing to her. Inge rightly assumed that this meant that Rudi knew nothing of the Captain's first letter to her. It so happened, Captain Thomas wrote, that his wife was at present staying at her parents' house in Oxford, and Jill would be welcome to stay there, and make this her base, and use it as her home address if she had need of one. If she and his wife took to each other, he wrote tactfully, they could go up to town together to meet Rudi's relations. Jill might like to consider the idea of being married from his parents-in-law's house; he hoped to arrange matters so that he would be able to be present as Rudi's best man.

She had borrowed books from the public library, by Havelock Ellis and others, to inform herself about homosexuality, and knew that even Oscar Wilde had been married and a father. She wondered if Rudi would always, in addition to a wife, need male partners. At this point she felt so dubious about him that she suspected him of not having told her the whole truth about Captain Thomas: as if she believed that Rudi's only value to another man could be as a catamite.

She thanked the Captain for his letter and told him that she needed time to decide. To Rudi she wrote, did they have to be quite so dependent on his relations? Supposing they waited until he was twenty-one which was not long, when they would no longer have to consider them at all but would be able to do as they pleased?

Alas, Rudi wrote back, had he not warned her that he was a dark sheep—or was the expression, a black horse? It made her wonder if he had really ever been as amusing as she had thought him. He wrote that for him, his twenty-first birthday would come and go without working magic changes: at the beginning of the war, when the Nazis with whom he had been interned had almost killed him (she had by now seen his scars), his dear relations, in exchange for rescuing him, had extracted a signature from him which meant that he would not be financially independent until he was thirty. He could not pretend to have forgotten to mention it to her—he had lacked the courage—he could only abjectly grovel. But the money was there true enough and his relations were known to be very generous to their own—which she would be once she became his wife.

Before she could answer this he wrote again to say that he had good news and bad news for her. The good news was that his commission was coming through—it would look so much better if he could stand under the *chupah* in subaltern's uniform, didn't she agree? Inge felt so remote from him that she took this at face value and felt that he was disappointing her. The bad news was that his relations were suggesting that, in view of wartime shortages and the fact that he would have to be away from home, their marriage endowment, meant to buy and furnish a house, should remain invested for the duration while she made her home with them. Had she decided on her wedding-dress? And not to forget that the maids would see what underwear she possessed when they unpacked for her.

They were to be married on his next leave.

While this correspondence was going on she had a letter from Hamish. He had written a poem about Sebastian's death but hesitated to send it to her—did she wish him to do so? When he had first told her that he, too, wrote poetry, she had rather despised him for it, thinking it as unsuitable an occupation for a man as looking after babies—just what you might expect of someone who refused to fight Hitler. When she read some of his poems, and wished she had written them, it did not occur to her that this might mean that she was aspiring to a masculine talent; it made her think of him as effeminate, as at best no better than herself which was not saying much for him. She felt that she had enough to cope with, without reliving Sebastian's death or being confronted with her life's ambition; she wrote to Hamish that he ought not to send her anything just now, she would be changing her address as she was getting married and she was very busy.

Hamish's response made her feel even more uneasy than the worst of Rudi's letters had done: it was so conventional that it made her ask herself, oh, Mutti, am I still me? Who was the lucky man? he enquired. She saw no reason for not telling him.

It brought her a letter from Hansi, pages and pages of it in her self-satisfied arrogant scrawl: the writing of someone who thought nothing of trampling on people, more a man's than her brother's; shockingly wasteful of paper—in wartime!—Inge thought, as if she were Miss Pym. "I am a shit," Hansi began— as Dolph might have done—a no-good future sister-in-law, she still hoped—and what was that supposed to mean? Inge wondered. She had promised David to look after her and it had been a real promise, not extracted but freely given. But Inge remembered that Hansi had once said that the way to David's heart lay through his sister. "If he ever knew . . ." she wrote, which Inge assumed to mean not, if he comes back, but when he comes back, don't tell him . . . . Shit though she was, she had made a point of spending her last leave in Leeds but Inge had been as prickly as a hedgehog, and like a shit, instead of taking the trouble to get at her soft underbelly . . . Hansi had no sense of the fitness of words, Inge thought as she read this. Her only excuse was that her friend had had problems—written in English, this did not divulge which one of her friends it had been.

Anyway, Hansi wrote, unnecessarily starting a fresh sheet, with writing that shouted, Inge could most certainly not marry Rudi: he was a homosexual, David had told her so. Suspecting Hansi of lacking reticence, Inge wondered if the Dolphin did not know that Rudi loved him, or if he knew, what it meant that he had kept it from Hansi as he had from herself. The fact, Hansi wrote, that Inge did not know this about Rudi was proof, if proof were needed, that he was totally unsuitable as a husband; Inge must break off their engagement at once and have nothing more to do with him. Of course she had had enough of her lonely life in Leeds: why did she not go and join Hamish on his baby-farm? The two of them were sure to get on like a house on fire; he had told Hansi that it came through in her every word that she was a girl after his own heart.

So angry that she was weeping, Inge wrote back that the fact that she was David's little sister did not mean that she was still little, she was quite as able as she needed to be to manage without her parents and her brother—and her brother's friends. Hansi knew nothing about her and her attempt to direct her life was, say, as if a traffic policeman were trying to direct a medieval pageant. Had Hansi never heard of mock marriages—*Scheinehen*, she translated as if Hansi's English were not as good as her own, an insult which was doubtlessly lost on Hansi. Young Zionists in Germany had gone in for it, she reminded her, to beat the British immigration quota. Her marriage with Rudi was not meant to be more than that. As a soldier's wife she would get an allowance to live on and she would no longer be classified as an enemy alien. The idea had originally been Sebastian's, but he had been killed before he could marry her—if Hansi did not know about that, that only showed that they should call themselves acquaintances rather than friends. What Rudi would get out of it would be enough money—how was too tedious to explain—to be able to afford to become an officer. She herself meant to settle in Oxford and prepare herself for matriculating as a student there.

That final sentence reconciled her to Rudi.

Within the week, she had a letter from Hamish, telling her that he would be in Leeds on the following Sunday, and the name of the hotel, and that he would be there all day; if she could not make it he would appreciate it if she would telephone him. It did not occur to her that he meant, so that he could persuade her to come.

She despised him for—as she thought—pretending that he suddenly had business in Leeds, when the truth was that he did not wish to force himself on her; she thought, the weekend is the only time when he can get away—when he had chosen it because Sunday was her free day. She usually got herself breakfast in bed and stayed there reading until noon, and then, while all the families in the land each got together over roast beef and Yorkshire pudding—except for those who were in the services and they would all be getting together too—she, unless the weather was too forbidding, went for a walk until the kitchen was free. She got her fire going and her cleaning and washing and cooking done, all in one go, which she thought of as Jill being Inge's Sunday skivvy. Every Sunday it was a toss-up with her which was worse: to stay in alone or to go to the pictures and have to come back to where no one was waiting for her.

There had been occasions when she had wished that she could meet Hamish: every time a letter from him conjured him up no more precisely than tomorrow's weather. But she was damned if they were going to meet because Hansi wanted it, had transparently wanted it for a long time: let Hamish submit to being bullied by her—and what sort of a man did that make him?— Inge would not! He might at least have enquired first if that Sunday suited her.

She lay in her bed and thought about him shallowly but more persistently than she had ever done before: usually, if he was in her mind it was as some piece of writing. They had been intellectually intimate for more than a year and she believed that she knew about him all that mattered.

The truth, which she would not admit to herself, was that just then she felt closer to him than to Rudi—from whom she felt more cut off than she had done the previous summer when he had stopped writing to her. Rudi had warned her that all men must fail her: because she would try to substitute them, as was only natural, for her brother—and it was in the nature of things that brothers could not be everything to their sisters. It was no mere coincidence, he argued, that she had fallen in love with a homosexual.

"But what about Sebastian?" she had asked—as not many brides could have done without provoking a rumpus, she thought, counting her blessings. Sebastian had been a self-made victim, Rudi maintained, and she had loved him as being beyond her reach; she would always love someone beyond her reach and when he was that no longer she would cease to love him.

Oh, for the prospects of a happy life, she thought, who would not rather be Joachim Meyer?

She got up, but only to go to the lavatory, and to go to the Dolphin's attic to fetch his bear; it was a long time since it had shared her bed; she needed someone to talk to. She would skip breakfast, saving both her rations and money, and let Hansi's brother buy her lunch.

She waited until the last minute before getting up, and then decided that she had left it too late: she could not show up as if she needed a free meal, it would be too embarrassing; it would be too embarrassing to make each other's acquaintance with their mouths full. She could have her breakfast for lunch and it would still be a saving. But first she had a bath and decided that her hair needed washing, which meant lighting the fire so that she would not be cold; and once the fire had been lit she did not want to go out so as not to waste the coal. As far as the corner, to phone him, before it got dark? Rudi was to tell her that she had been performing her courtship ritual: reducing her partner to a victim so that she could feel his equal. Had she spared no thought, he was to ask her, for poor Hamish biting his nails in his hotel bedroom?

It had occurred to her that he might come after her—that was how she thought of it, as if the pacifist were a predator and her furnished room not sufficiently her home ground to give her the advantage. She spent an hour or more of the early afternoon looking out of her bay window at the indifferent street, the bleak and rain-sodden park, wondering of every possible passer-by—there were not all that many young men in mufti—are you Hansi's brother? She grew unwilling to go out because he might waylay her. Forgotten were all the hundreds and thousands of words which his mind had released like pigeons to home on hers, make their home in hers; all she could think of was that he was someone she had never met who had expectations of her and would find her inadequate.

Aggrieved that even making a telephone call was more difficult for her now than it had been in her childhood, she thought that he probably believed, like Rudi's relations, that she

177

had a telephone in her flat, all hers, and went to the hairdressers' whenever her hair needed washing; it would serve him right, she thought, if she died of pneumonia because she went out to see him and resolved to go, at once, without even changing her light-blue jersey dress, half-price because it was shop-soiled, which made her feel like a sky-piece lost from a jigsaw puzzle. She did not own an umbrella and did not put up her hood—not to get it wet inside when her hair was wet already: it hung about her ears in a hundred ringlets but she was unaware that it made her look what an American would have called cute.

At the tram-stop, where she had to wait, and all the damp and dreary way into town she worked herself up into a rage, as if she had been summoned by Hitler; she stamped into the hotel and, thinking that it would shame him to be asked for by the likes of her, demanded at the reception desk, "Hamish Henderson!" Now there's camouflage for you, she thought. She was in such a state that she reverted to thinking of him as his father, one who had fought the British and been a prisoner of war; and when he was pointed out to her, on the far side of the lounge, standing as she had stood contemplating the drizzle, she thought, he's a real Prussian, holding himself so upright at his age! As if he could feel her looking at him he turned and she prayed, Oh, Sebastian, help me!

Because here was someone who could have taken Sebastian's place for her.

He was not at all as she had imagined him. He was younger, young, younger than Sebastian; he was tall—Hansi was tall for a girl—and lean; his hair was black as Hansi had said and he wore it rather long. In those days of military haircuts, it gave him a gipsy look; did Hansi not know the colour of her brother's—half-brother's—eyes or had she been unable to think of a rhyme for grey? they were slate-grey like Inge's own. His features were too irregular to be handsome but he had the kindest, most caring face she had ever seen; she wished that she were a little girl again so that she could run across the room and throw herself into his arms. I can't feel as I do about someone I haven't even yet met, she told herself, a year's correspondence working like yeast within her all the more

178

potently for having been forgotten. It isn't him, she told herself, inwardly screaming like a petrified rabbit.

He came towards her, looking not at the obstacles—people, furniture—between them but at her all the way, with his hands held out, though he dropped them before he reached her. "Good, you've come," he echoed Sebastian's words, boarding her life like a pirate. "Inge!" It seemed to her that it was a long time since anybody had called her that; he made it sound like a snatch of a Schubert song. "I rather thought that you would be like this," he said, looking into her so deeply that she felt ground between millstones into manna for the wilderness. She found that he had taken her hand after all, had held it, stroked it between his own: she was not really aware of it until it felt cold and naked after he had let go. "I'm sorry you had to come out on such a day," he said, and looked round for someone to take her behind the scenes and hand her a towel so that she could dry her hair. She almost said, I don't want to leave you, or some stupidity like that, and remembered that he was used to looking after small helpless things and that with him she was safe.

When she came back, his image on her retinas, she could not at once see him and felt shipwrecked, but there he was beside her, putting an arm about her shoulders, hugging her to him, saying, "Don't look so lost, ma wee lassie!" With his free hand, he indicated a window recess where a waitress was setting out their tea; he shepherded her towards it; where the gangway for them was too narrow, he withdrew his arm and took her hand instead.

They sat opposite each other and held hands across the table. He said, "I am sorry, I meant to let you have more time to get used to Sebastian's death . . ." He transferred his hold on her to his left hand so that he could pour their tea; he knew better than to ask her if she took it with milk.

He looked at her as one holds a match to something to set it alight and she could not bear it: looked down at his hand as if hands were a novelty to her, thinking that the saddest thing in the lives of his babies was not that they were orphaned or unwanted but that later in life they would not remember how he had tended them. He said, "I'm too much like you, Inge, I would just have let you go, I'm used to loving people and losing them.

Hansi can be a bit of an elephant, she told me to come because your brother would never forgive her if she didn't stop you, and I have been marshalling all the arguments. But they're none of them necessary, Inge, are they? We are—you know, Plato's two halves of the one egg? It's in Yeats." It occurred to her then that we love people not, or not only, for their sake but for our own: she liked herself well enough in Rudi's company, but she liked herself better with Hamish, with him she felt reconciled to being who she was.

"I've got to marry Rudi now," she told him, astounded to be feeling so light of heart: in an existence which included Hamish she could cope with anything. Just then, the waitress came back with a plateful of cakes; when she had gone Hamish asked, "What's that 'now' doing there, Inge?"

"It's nothing to do with you," she said, her tone conveying that what she meant was that it was not there because they had just met. "I mean now that he and his relations have come to expect it."

He withdrew his hand from her, gently, as if the gesture meant no more than that he needed it though he didn't: he made a steeple with his fingertips and leant back and said, "Tell me about it," as if it were a phrase he used often. When she had done explaining he said, "I've never heard such rubbish. He's not the only refugee to get a commission and they don't all have rich uncles. I am sorry to have to say this to you, Inge, but I think Rudi loves you, I think he just can't bring himself to admit it to you, or, more likely, from what you have told me, what he can't manage is admitting it to himself. Of course you have to marry him, it would destroy him if you didnt. You and I—*wir sind Stehaufmännchen*." (The English translation, tumbler-doll, fails to convey the idea of the manikin who refuses to stay knocked down.)

She loved him more than she had loved Sebastian who had believed that she needed his pity.

He offered his hand back to her, asking, "Do you think Rudi will mind if we hold hands?" She took it and told him, "He won't, he's very understanding, in many ways he is just right for me." But her eyes belied her words, said not to hurt but to reassure. Stroking the back of her hand with his thumb, he told her, "Just before I came away, I found a foster-mother for Fiona." She knew why he said it: to remind her that he was schooled in giving up those he loved to the love of others.

He said, "Don't cry, lassie, it doesn't do me any good to see you miserable. Your marriage to Rudi doesn't mean that we have to give each other up. That thought's not prompted by strength, lassie, but by weakness." She acknowledged the truth of this with a rainbow smile and he said, "If I must not hinder then I must help, there must be something I can do for you."

As if this were her reason for coming to him she said, "Tell me what I ought to do about Rudi's relations," and explained why they were a problem, finishing with her rejection of Mrs Thomas. "If she were there with me that would only mean being scared in two directions." He gazed at her, perhaps thinking of her being scared of people, while she imagined him being equally scared as a boy, and perhaps even now though he had learned—as she would learn—not to show it.

He asked, "Those foster-parents you had in the beginning, Johnnie and Rosie Sparrow, they wouldn't be posh enough?" and Inge told him, "I don't want them if I can't have my real parents." She fished in her handbag for her address book and handed it over, as she had not opened her wardrobe for Sebastian. He had hardly started looking when he asked her, "How do you come to know Jean Crowther?"

Inge explained that she had befriended the Dolphin since the Dovercourt reception camp. Hamish had known her for about as long, through the Peace Pledge Union. "We can both stay with her," he said. Inge looked at him round-eyed, believing for a moment that what he was suggesting was that they should go to London together and marry each other. "You'll not refuse to let me come to your wedding, lassie?" he asked. "You'll need to have somebody present as your family!"

She had the impulse to sweep the table between them clear with the back of her hand, or better still, to pick the things up one by one and throw them at him, beginning with the teapot, still hot and half full. She abhorred him with his, "I'm sorry, Inge, I'm sorry . . .", hated him as his father's people had taught her to hate because he would not put up a fight for her, not fight her, refused to take charge of her as if she were not just as orphaned and unwanted as his babies. She thought, I suppose he thinks I'm an adult . . .

Hatred of him carried her through their parting. When he telephoned the home, in the evening, as he had arranged, he was told that the man who had been left in charge had had a stroke, or the man's father had had one—afterwards Inge was not sure, she could not make herself listen to him once she realized that he was going to leave her for the sake of those babies, who passed in and out of his life by the dozen without even knowing it; yet she would have despised him for it if he had thought her more important than his work. He had meant to stay long enough to give her time to pack, and to take her back with him; it felt to her as if rage were melting her bones when she understood that before even seeing her he had made plans for them both, had taken her agreement for granted as if she belonged to him—and now without even consulting her was changing his mind because, he said, of the changed circumstances. It wasn't her circumstances that had changed.

"I'm sorry, Inge," he said, looking at his watch and chewing at his lip because he was lying to her, was not sorry at all but eager to get away: because he knew that what she wanted to do was to abandon Rudi and that when she calmed down and realized it she would get him to help her to make that decision—and for ever afterwards resent him as the cause of her doing something for which she would not be able to forgive herself.

If he was to catch the night train there was not even time for him to see her home. That suited him well: he was not at all sure that he would have been able to resist the temptation of going in with her to show her what it was that she had dismissed as "of no importance unless you want to have children, and who would want that when Hitler is winning the war?" Their leave-taking was encumbered with her protestations that she did not need a taxi and that if she was taking one then he did not need to pay for it. They were not parting for ever: would meet again in less than a fortnight, at the wedding.

It was an expensive taxi ride, and before it was over the reaction had set in. When she thought of Hamish, who was so nice, so caring, travelling back on his own to all his responsibilities, she wanted to take him into her arms less to hug him than to protect him from she knew not what. She thought of him as constantly expending himself on so many people and having no one, being so alone that even having her would have made a difference. Oh, Hamish! she thought, her heart going out to him.

But then she thought, Oh, Rudi!

For more than half the night, she lay awake, and swung like a pendulum between the two young men, because there was no getting round the problem of wanting more the one whom she had rejected. Twice she got up to write a letter: the first one, to Rudi, did not get beyond an account of her meeting with Hamish because she could not make herself write that she no longer wanted to marry him; in the second letter, to Hamish, she suggested that after getting married she should come to work for him. It seemed an ideal solution, until she remembered Hamish's comment that Rudi loved her and, striving to see the arrangement through Rudi's eyes, realized that it looked very much like doing things by halves.

Her last thought before falling asleep, long after midnight, was that it was absurd that she, whose greatest problem had always been that she wasn't necessary, should suddenly be needed by two young men at once.

Rudi now wrote to her almost daily and that Monday morning, too, it was the sound of the post arriving that got her out of bed; but the thickness of the envelope made her quail: he ought not, at this stage, to have so much to say to her that could not wait until he came to pick her up for the journey south and their wedding—if she was going to go through with it.

"Oh, Rudi!" she said under her breath on seeing the disorganisation of his handwriting, it made her want to hold him in her arms, to reassure him. Oxford or Cambridge, he wrote, were out for her, his relations had vetoed the idea. Rightly she would think that they might have waited until she could put her case, but this was how they did things in the family and she would have to get used to it, like milk in her tea; this reminder of Dovercourt made her feel, as it was meant to do, that Rudi and she had come a long way together. For once, he wrote, he had to agree with them: at Oxford or Cambridge she would not fit in twice over: once because she did not share the background of the people who went there, and once as a girl—another university would be better. He was to be stationed for the foreseeable future near Edinburgh, which had a university which took in lots of girls and was said to welcome foreigners; his relations questioned the wisdom of her decision to study English but were not going to insist on her changing her mind.

"Oh, thank you very much," Inge said as if she had always been in the position of taking going to university for granted, and turned to the next page.

He had been to Edinburgh, Rudi wrote, and liked it. It had a castle, which from a distance looked more spectacular than it was, but a distance was where she would see it from as it had been taken over by the military. And Princes Street had the reputation of being one of the finest streets in the world. Like Hamburg, Edinburgh had a port and a zoo and to that extent already made him feel at home; he hoped that the Pentland Hills would serve to make her feel at home, too.

Alas, his relations would not let them have their marriage portion, arguing that they would need it after the war to set up house in London. But the property-owning side of the firm was buying a house—or had bought it already, he wasn't sure— which they would be able to live in at a nominal rent, and did she think that would do? Not daring to believe that she had understood what she had just read she glanced ahead and saw that there was more about the house: but he was only apologizing that she had not been given a say in the choice, and explaining that they would be able to buy the most essential things with the cheque they would get at their wedding.

Would she settle for Edinburgh to settle in? It wasn't far from Glasgow, so it should not be difficult for her to run away from him to her friend Hamish . . .

"Oh, Rudi!" she exclaimed aloud, reassured, willing, finally, to settle for Rudi.

He understood her better than she did herself: had taken great care to word his letter in such a way that instead of resenting that she was not getting what she wanted she was welcoming what she was getting, with the feeling that it was more than she had the right to expect.